CW01203352

This is a work of Fiction. All charact
although based in historical settings. If
the story it is a coincidence.

Credits

Thanks to: My wife who is so supportive and believed in me. My dogs and cats who watch me act out the fight scenes and must wonder what the hell has gotten into their boss. Finally, to all those who provided feedback on all those annoying typos and spelling mistakes.

The Dorset Boy Series Timeline

1792 – 1795   Book 1: A Talent for Trouble
Marty joins the Navy as an Assistant Steward and ends up a midshipman.

1795 – 1798   Book 2: The Special Operations Flotilla
Marty is a founder member of the Special Operations Flotilla, learns to be a spy and passes as lieutenant.

1799 – 1802   Book 3: Agent Provocateur
Marty teams up with Linette to infiltrate Paris, marries Caroline, becomes a father and fights pirates in Madagascar.

1802 – 1804   Book 4: In Dangerous Company
Marty and Caroline are in India helping out Arthur Wellesley, combating French efforts to disrupt the East India Company and French sponsored pirates on Reunion. James Stockley born

1804 – 1805   Book 5: The Tempest
Piracy in the Caribbean, French interference, Spanish gold and the death of Nelson. Marty makes Captain.

1806 – 1807   Book 6: Vendetta

A favour carried out for a prince, a new ship, the S.O.F. move to Gibraltar, the battle of Maida, counter espionage in Malta and a Vendetta declared and closed.

1807 – 1809   Book 7: The Trojan Horse

Rescue of the Portuguese royal family, Battle of the Basque Roads with Thomas Cochrane, and back to the Indian Ocean and another conflict with the French Intelligence Service.

1809 – 1811   Book 8: La Licorne

Marty takes on the role of Viscount Wellington's Head of Intelligence. Battle of The Lines of Torres Vedras, siege of Cadiz, skulduggery, espionage and blowing stuff up to confound the French.

1812   Book 9: Raider

Marty is busy. From London to Paris to America and back to the Mediterranean for the battle of Salamanca. A mission to the Adriatic reveals a white slavery racket that results in a private mission to the Caribbean to rescue his children.

1813-1814   Book 10: Silverthorn

Promoted to Commodore and given a Viscountcy Marty is sent to the Caribbean to be Governor of Aruba which provides the cover story he needs to fight American privateers and undermine the Spanish in South America. On his return he escorts Napoleon into Exile on Alba.

1815-1816   Book 11: Exile

After 100 days in exile Napoleon returns to France and Marty tries to hunt him down. After the battle of Waterloo Marty again escorts him into Exile on St Helena. His help is requested by the Governor of Ceylon against the rebels in Kandy.

Contents

Chapter 1: Back To The Mast

Martin Stockley, midshipman on his Majesty's ship Falcon, a sixth-rate frigate currently completing her refit in Portsmouth, stepped off the post chase from London and took a deep breath of sea air. It was late June 1795, and it looked to be shaping up into a pleasant summer. Portsmouth smelled far better than London even with the docks pervading the air with the scent of rotting garbage and other unspeakable things that people thought if they threw into the water would just disappear. All that happened in reality is all the garbage just washed back and forth on the tide and didn't go anywhere.

He retrieved his sea chest and paid a porter to take it to the George Hotel where he would stay until he would re-join his ship in a couple of days. She was currently having her masts stepped after an extensive refit and, once that was done, he would boat over and take his place back in the cockpit with the other Mids.

His time in London had been spent in the London home of the Count de Marchets and his family, who were refugees from the French Revolution. He had been fortunate to be instrumental in their escape from Toulon just before the city was overrun by the revolutionaries and was treated as a favoured nephew. The Count's daughter, Contessa Evelyn, and Martin were firm friends. He had felt attracted to her in a way that threatened to go beyond friendship as she was becoming a beautiful young woman, but he wasn't ready for that just yet.

He had also run into Armand, a French Navy officer and spy, who he had accompanied on a secret mission in Marseille. He had introduced him to William Wickham, who was someone important in the English Security Service. They had talked about his adventures in Marseille and Toulon and talked in French. They had complimented him on his mastery of the language but said he needed to work on his accent as he had a definite Basque twang.

Wickham had asked him what he thought of the experience, and he had answered honestly that he found it exciting but was frustrated he couldn't have been a more active participant. The two men laughed at that and exchanged a knowing look.

He arrived at the hotel and entered the common room, which was full of Naval officers waiting to join ships or looking for a ship to join. He had sent a message ahead to book a room, so, when he arrived, he just announced his arrival to the nearest member of staff, waited to receive his key, and arranged for a servant to take his chest to his room.

He was about to go up when he was hailed from the bar. His fellow midshipman, Patrick Mulhoon, was calling him over to a group of their peers stood at the bar drinking beer. Mulhoon was seventeen years old and one of Martin's best friends on the Falcon.

"Gentlemen," he said in his soft Irish accent, "may I introduce Mr. Martin (Marty to his friends) Stockley, a shipmate on the Falcon and a proper fighting sailor." He grabbed Marty by the arm and drew him into the crowd.

"So, you are the famous Marty,'" said a tall lad of around 18 years old with a refined accent who pronounced Marty 'Martee' in a French accent.

"James Hepworth, late of the Victory and now of the Frigate Surprise." He introduced himself and held out his hand, which Marty shook as he blushed bright pink.

"We had the pleasure of the Count de Marchets and his delightful daughter on our voyage back from Gibraltar. We were all smitten and trying to woo the beautiful Contessa," he added with a sly wink. Marty bristled but then James continued, "but to no avail as she had already been smitten with her ''ero Martee', who had gallantly and singlehandedly rescued the fair maid not once, but twice!" He grinned at Marty, who stammered that it wasn't single-handed, and he was sure she exaggerated it all . . . really.

The boys laughed and slapped him on the back. James ordered him a beer and asked him,

"What really happened, then?"

Marty started telling his version, but Patrick took over saying he was being too modest and gave an exaggerated and extremely blood thirsty account, dwelling on the knife and tomahawk killings. After that, he had to show them his fighting knife and let them hold it. A young mid from the Circe even managed to cut himself, much to everyone's amusement.

Later, alone in his room looking out over the harbour with a swimming head from a couple of beers too many, Marty wondered why there were so many Frigates in port at the same time. They were the workhorses of the fleet and there were never enough of them. So why were they here?

The papers had been full of the Battle of Genoa where Admiral Hoffam and elements of the Neapolitan fleet had defeated a French fleet, capturing two French ships. In his opinion, he agreed with Nelson that it was a bit of a nothing battle, and an opportunity had been lost for a much bigger victory.

He woke up with a headache, "serves you right," he said to himself in the mirror as pair of red rimmed, bloodshot eyes looked back at him. He dressed and went down to the common room for breakfast. As he entered, he saw a familiar face at a table by the window.

"Hello Richard," he said to Lieutenant Richard Dicky, Fourth Lieutenant of the Falcon, "didn't know you were staying here."

"I'm not," he replied, rising, and shaking Marty's hand.

"I'm berthed on board. I came ashore to find you and Mulhoon. Our schedule has been brought forward and the captain wants you onboard. As the breakfast here is one of the best in Portsmouth, I decided to take advantage and get one in. Join me."

They settled down to a large breakfast from a buffet set up on the bar. They filled their plates from a selection of kippers, kidneys, devilled eggs, fried eggs, lamb chops, sausages, mashed potatoes, bacon, bread, butter, honey, jam, marmalade, tea, and coffee.

As only young men can, they chowed down and cleared a prodigious amount of food. After about an hour, they exchanged belches, Marty asked the hosteler to rouse Mr. Mulhoon and to have both of their sea chests brought down as they had to join their ship immediately.

Mulhoon sat beside Marty in the middle of the gig with his head in his hands and groaned. He hadn't had the benefit of a huge calorie laden breakfast or copious amounts of coffee, so he was getting the full effect of mixing beer and brandy the night before. Richard Dicky took great delight in steering the boat over the worst of the waves in a way that caused it to rock and pitch to make him feel even worse. They eventually arrived at the Falcon and jokingly asked him if they needed to get a chair rigged to sling him onboard. Mulhoon manfully stood and climbed the battens up the side to gain the deck, but his misery didn't stop there. The ship was a mass of shouting, hammering, sawing, swearing and worse, the smell of paint and tar. It even made Marty wince.

The First Lieutenant, Mr. Hill, approached, took one look at Mulhoon, and told him to get below and report on deck when he was able to work. He then cast an eye over Marty seeing the bloodshot eyes but noting that he stood erect and wasn't too green around the gills.

"Get into your slops Mr. Stockley and take charge of your division. They are helping erect the rigging on the foremast. We want this ship ready to sail in record time." He looked along the deck then back at Marty, "Are you still here?" Marty snapped a salute and said, "No sir," and ran for the ladder down to the cockpit.

His division looked pleased to see him. They had been under the command of a bosun's mate who was a meddler. He didn't let them get on with their work, which they all knew how to do, but kept stopping them to describe the next step of the operation. Marty asked the mate what the task was then told him to 'go find something else to do as he would take care of it now' and 'thank you for your efforts'.

He looked at his men and said, "Now, will you men get on with raising that cathead up to the top of the mast, or am I going to have to call the steps?"

"We be on it, Mr. Stockley!" shouted John Smith the fourth (John Smith the third had ruptured himself and had to be put ashore so John had gone from the fifth to the fourth now).

The ship's fiddler was grinding out 'Jack's the Lad' from atop the capstan, and the men picked up the beat to coordinate the heave. From then on, the work went easy. Marty told them what he wanted doing and they did it, unless, of course, none of them had done it before and then they would talk it over with Marty or he would consult with a mate or another officer if necessary. Marty watched and learned. He didn't assume he knew better than the men just because he had a higher rank.

A week of hard work saw them ready to bring the guns aboard. The Falcon's hull had been strengthened with new knees and re-enforcements to the gun deck. She was being rearmed with twenty-six new eighteen pounders rather than the twenty-eight nine pounders she had before. They were also fitting a pair of brass long nines as bow chasers and four six pounders on the quarterdeck making her up to a thirty-two-gun ship. That, of course, didn't include the six thirty-two-pound carronades, two at the bow on the fore deck and four on the quarterdeck that gave her a devastating close in punch. Marty made sure his beloved carronades were installed correctly and that their gun crews took personal responsibility for their installation. The Falcon now had one hell of a punch and a full two-hundred-and-fifty-man crew.

In the evenings when the work stopped, Marty found Roland du Demaine, engaged him in conversation, and he, in turn, pulled in the other Frenchmen. As they talked, Marty's vocabulary increased, and he learned to speak with not only a Parisian accent but the one from Lyon as well. Quite accidently, he also absorbed information about the hometowns of the three Frenchmen and lots of little facts about the way of life in France.

After all the guns were installed, they started provisioning the ship. The first lieutenant and the captain were carefully planning the location of the stores so that not only was the ship trimmed perfectly when she was fully laden but as the stores were used, the trim would be maintained. Marty oversaw the stores coming onboard and kept a record of what and how many that would be passed to Mr. Evans, the purser.

The Falcons were lucky they had that rare bird that was an honest purser, who was actually liked by the crew. He was making a fair profit, but he didn't rob them blind or cheat them in the process. When the salt beef and pork was delivered, Evans inspected the dates and condition of every one of the casks. He rejected, out of hand, a complete delivery where the casks were dated 1767. He wasn't having nearly thirty-year-old salt beef on his ship! That caused a visit from the provisioning officer, who came prepared to read the riot act to Evans, but for some reason, walked away without saying a word when Evans said something quietly in his ear just after he boarded. Marty strongly suspected Evans knew something the provisioning officer didn't want made public.

Next came the water hoys and the taking on of tons of fresh water stored in casks that were brand new and had been commissioned by the captain at his own cost. Personal stores and livestock came onboard last.

They warped the ship out of the dock and towed her over to the powder dock. This was the most dangerous part of the whole provisioning as they hoisted a full load of powder down into the magazine. No naked flames, absolutely no smoking, and all metal objects that could cause sparks put away. The deck was sanded and wetted to catch any stray powder grains that may have leaked and thoroughly washed down afterwards.

After that, they went for a short shakedown cruise to check that nothing fell off or broke and that everything worked as it was supposed to. They even fired off the guns to check the tackles worked just so. When they returned to Portsmouth, Captain Turner reported them ready for sea in all respects.

Typically, they heard nothing for almost a week.

Chapter 2: The Danish Patrol

A boat with a midshipman onboard approached the Falcon on Tuesday, June the 16th with dispatches. After he left, Captain Turner called his lieutenants to his quarters for a briefing. When they came out, the First started preparing the ship to sail, and Marty got a chance to ask Richard Dicky where they were going,

"The Downs," was the reply.

"The Downs??" Said Marty.

"Yes, The Downs. We are to proceed there with all dispatch, and we will receive new orders when we get there. Damn strange if you ask me," replied Richard.

"We are to meet the Reunion, Vestel, and Isis there and place ourselves under the command of Captain James Alms of the Reunion. That is all I know."

Marty had to go down to the hold and was passing through the orlop deck when he bumped into Evans the Purser.

"Are you going down into the hold Martin?" asked Evans.

"Aye, Mr. Evans. I'm to inventory the shot store," Marty replied. It wasn't a glamorous job but needed to be done.

"Then I will accompany you as what I need to check on is in that area as well," said Evans.

As they made their way forward holding Lanthorns for light, Evans asked,

"Did you get to see your family while you were on shore?"

"Aye, I did. Pop died before I got back but mum is fine, and I got to see the new babies of my brothers and sisters."

Evans put his hand on his arm to stop him and looked him in the eye.

"You don't have much in common with them anymore, do you?" he said.

"No, everything's changed. Well, they're the same but I'm different to them now," he said sadly.

"Well now, that's as maybe son, but family is forever, and they will be as proud as punch of what you be doing. Don't stay away from them no matter what happens as they be the only family you will ever get!" Marty realised that had been just what he had been thinking of doing as he had felt so – separated – that was the word – from his family. Everything had changed, and he didn't know how to deal with it.

"You be right," he told Evans, "I can't expect them to understand how I've changed or why but damn it, they be mine own."

"Good lad," said Evans, "Now, let's get down into that hold."

Marty got on with his inventory feeling better in himself, while Evans rummaged around searching for whatever he had come down for.

"Marty," called Evans, "can you give me a hand getting this crate open?"

Marty noted where he had got to and made his way to the glow of Evan's lanthorn. He found the purser tugging at a large crate trying to get it out into the space between the stacks. Marty took the other side of it, heaved it clear, then got a prybar and levered off the lid. To his surprise, it looked like the crate was full of fabric.

Evans reached in and grabbed the top item and pulled it out. Once he had unfolded it, he could see it was a heavy sailor's jacket.

What the hell do he need those for it be just coming in to summer, thought Marty.

"Thank you, Marty. This is what I was looking for," said Evans and shooed him back to his work.

They got underway on the afternoon tide and that evening at dinner all the talk in the cockpit was about the upcoming voyage. They all knew they were going to The Downs, and they had to explain to the youngest mid, Cecil, that the Downs were just off the East coast of Kent near Deal. The speculation ranged from attacking Amsterdam, as the Dutch Republic had succumbed to the French in the winter and was now known as the Batavian Republic, to sailing into the Baltic and patrolling there.

After dinner, as none of the mids were on duty, Bob Graveny got out a guitar and started to play well-known songs that they could all sing along to. Simon Clegg pulled out a flute and played along most competently to the surprise of all the other mids. Marty contributed a bottle from his store of wine, and they all had a merry time.

It was a pretty boring trip round the coast to The Downs and when they got there, they found the other three frigates already there. They came to anchor and Captain Taylor was taken across to the Reunion. When he returned, he called a conference to tell his officers what they were about to embark on.

"Gentlemen," he said once they were all gathered in his cabin. "We are to be part of a squadron formed by the Reunion, Vestel, Isis, and us that will patrol the Danish Norwegian coast to ensure that our supply lines from the Nordics are kept open. This is vital to the Fleet as this is our main source of Stockholm tar and timber. Our patrol area will be the Skagerrak, which for those unfamiliar with the Nordics, is a strait running between the Southeast coast of Norway, the Southwest coast of Sweden, and the Jutland Peninsula, which is part of Denmark, Mr. Braithwaite." The mids and younger lieutenants laughed at that and the Mini-Mid, as he was known, blushed furiously.

"We will leave on the eighth of August, weather permitting. I want all of you to familiarize yourselves with the charts of the area and the capabilities of Dutch warships. We've not come across them before. Our mission is important, our Navy depends on it."

For the next few days, they prepared for the voyage North. That time of the year they wouldn't be faced with extreme cold, but they were used to Mediterranean temperatures and the conditions in the Skagerrak would challenge them until they acclimatised. Now, Marty knew why the purser was looking for those winter jackets.

August the eighth dawned bright and clear with a wind coming straight up the channel from the South. They could see a big bank of cloud to the West, so expected it to veer more Westerly later.

The signal to make sail came as soon as the tide was right. They formed up in line astern, with the Falcon first, the Reunion second, Vestel third, and Isis last, being the smallest.

It seemed that all four ships were announcing their presence in the loudest possible way by holding live fire practice on the great guns for an hour a day. It was necessary on the Falcon as the eighteens had a crew of ten and the new gun crews had to get to know each other. The captain also practiced evolutions with the guns where he would randomly point at crewmen or a gun and declare them wounded, killed or out of action. The remaining crew were expected to adapt and make sure the broadside continued at maximum efficiency.

Fourteen days later, they were approaching the mouth of the Skagerrak when the Mainmast lookout called out,

"Sail Ho!! Two points off the starboard bow!"

Midshipman Mulhoon was sent up as he had very sharp eyes and he soon announced that there were two ships that he could see from their Topsails, and they were probably Frigates.

Captain Turner said.

"Signal 'Enemy in Sight' then 'Two Frigates North Northeast'."

"Sir, Reunion signalling," cried Midshipman Clegg, who was on signal duty. "Our Number." A pause as he consulted the signal book. "Make more sail, Engage the Enemy more closely."

"HA! Make more sail, he says," laughed Captain Turner, "Let's have as much canvas as she will bear, Mr. Hill. We have a clean bottom now, so let's see how fast she can go!"

They soon slowly started to outpace the ships behind them as they homed in on the foreign sails and it wasn't long before another hail came from the masthead.

"Deck there! I can see three ships; two frigates and a cutter hull up. They have seen us, are turning away, and making sail. Heading Northwest. I think they are Batavian."

Marty was at his carronades, so was well positioned to hear everything on the quarterdeck.

"Master! The chart please," called the captain, and he and the master poured over it, discussing in low voices.

"They must be heading for Egeroe," he finally declared, "that's a neutral Danish port, and they can hide in there."

"Mr. Hill, how fast are we catching them?"

Hill consulted a slate he had been calculating on.

"At this range, I can only estimate that we are gaining at around 1 knot," he reported.

"We are logging 12 knots and a fathom right now, sir."

"Wet down the sails and run out the stunsails. We will squeeze 13 knots yet," ordered Captain Turner.

Time dragged by but eventually Mr. Hill and the Master were able to take a sight off the top of the enemy's mast. They could work out an exact range by using trigonometry. They knew the height of the mast and the angle so could work out the range and by taking one sighting every fifteen minutes, they were able to calculate that the Falcon was gaining at just over two knots. As the rearmost ship of the enemy squadron was now hull up from the quarterdeck, they all knew that they were no more than seven miles or about three hours behind.

The crew were served lunch, and they went to action stations when they were about thirty minutes behind them. At just about four o'clock in the afternoon, they were close enough to try the bow chasers. The captain blew his horn, the hunt was on!

"She is the Alliante, sir," reported Mulhoon after another trip up the mast.

"Dutch built," said the Master, "I seen her back in 1789 when I was in Amsterdam. She be a thirty-six with twelve pounders as her mains if I remember rightly."

"We should have the measure of her. We throw a greater weight of iron, and I am sure we will have a greater rate of fire as well," said Mr. Hill.

"Indeed," said the Master, "but them Dutch do make a strong ship."

The bow chasers fired for the third time and a rip appeared in the Alliante's mizzen mainsail, costing her speed.

"She's going to make a fight of it!" exclaimed the captain as the Alliante took in her mains and reduced sail to fighting trim of Topsails and Royals only.

"Reduce sail to Topsails and Royals," the captain ordered "if they want a fight, they can have it."

"The rest of our ships are taking up the chase of the other two sir," shouted Cecil Braithwaite from the stern rail where he had been positioned to watch for signals.

"Signal from Isis, sir. 'Good Hunting'," reported Clegg

"Make 'God speed,' Mr. Clegg," ordered the captain and blew his horn.

"Larboard guns ready, sir," reported Richard Dickey.

Here we go, thought Marty as the Alliante swung her bow to starboard to bring her broadside to bear.

For what we are about to receive... and she fired.

Thirty-six, twelve-pound balls screamed across the deck, the Dutch had double shot their guns but fired high. The Falcon's guns boomed their reply. It was a quarter after four, and the two ships were now broadside to broadside.

Broadside after broadside was fired by both ships and soon, the sea flattened, and the breeze died, blown away by the concussion of the cannon.

Marty's smashers were in full cry, and he was ordered to concentrate on the rigging to disable the Dutchman while the main guns did their deadly work on the hull. After thirty minutes, the guns were so hot that they were jumping back on the recoil and the men had to be extra careful not to get caught by them.

Men were wounded by flying splinters or shot. The number nine eighteen-pounder suffered a direct hit with four of her crew injured and two killed. The men were loading and firing automatically, too stunned by the noise and exhausted by the continual firing to do anything other.

Then after an hour at a quarter past five, the Alliante struck. Her captain finally admitting that he was outgunned and outnumbered as the squadron were returning, having given up the chase as the other Batavian Frigate and Cutter made it into the harbour.

The butcher's bill on the Falcon was three dead and fourteen wounded with one not expected to survive the night. On boarding the Alliante, they found she had nine dead and twenty-seven wounded including a lieutenant who was killed when an eighteen-pound ball passed very close to his head and the shockwave took his life without leaving a mark on him.

The Dutch sailors were disarmed and imprisoned in the hold and cable tier. The officers either gave their parole or were disarmed and imprisoned away from the sailors in the brig.

Captain Alms wanted all his frigates to continue the patrol, so he created a prize crew from men from all four ships commanded by Lieutenant Hill of the Falcon. Dispatches were entrusted to Lieutenant William Huggell of the Reunion who joined the Alliante as super cargo. Marty was chosen from the mids to go on the prize because his leadership qualities and independence made him the most useful to Hill. Unsurprisingly, Tom Savage, John Smith the fourth, and his four Basques all managed to finagle a way on to the prize as well.

After repairs, they left the squadron on the twenty-fifth of August and headed back to Spithead. It was an uneventful three-week trip, the Dutch prisoners were well behaved and were, in turn, treated well by the English sailors.

On arrival in Spithead, Huggell immediately set off to the admiralty, and Hill waited to see what his orders would bring. He had hope that he would get command of the Alliante if she was bought in. The prize crew waited on board for a ship to come and take them back to the squadron.

Chapter 3: Transfer

Two weeks went by and November arrived with a winter storm that even affected the anchored ships in Spithead. It was still going strong after two days when a boat approached the Alliante with a very wet midshipman in the stern. He managed to board without falling in, despite the efforts of the choppy sea, with dispatches and a sea chest. He went straight down to the captain's cabin to Lieutenant Hill.

Marty was surprised to hear a call for him to attend Hill in his cabin and hurried down to be announced by the Marine at the door. He was even more surprised when the wet mid. handed him a dispatch of his own, much to Hill's obvious annoyance.

He examined the seal and saw the admiralty's fouled anchor on it, and carefully opened it. It was a big occasion to get your first personal dispatch after all, and he was savouring every moment. He quickly skip-read the standard preamble to the heart of the message.

You are hereby required to report to the office of Admiral Lord Hood at The Admiralty on the tenth November in the AM for assignment on a special duty. You will select six men from the crew of the Falcon to accompany you. These men to be fit for duty and rated able.

"Well, I'm damned," he said and read it again to make sure he hadn't misread it. He also noted it had been signed by the Secretary to the First Naval Lord.

"Well? What does it say?" demanded Hill. Marty told him and then handed over the paper for him to read.

"Astonishing," said Hill, "I am instructed to return on the Derbyshire to the Squadron with the prize crew and Mr. Stokes to replace you. You are ordered to London for a special duty. I don't suppose you have any idea what it is?"

Marty shook his head.

"Well, you had better get ready to leave. I don't suppose I need to ask which six men you will take with you as your cutthroats are all on board." Marty grinned at him as he took his orders back and folded them carefully.

"Aye, Tom Savage and the boys will be coming with me. I couldn't stop them if I wanted to."

Marty went straight out to tell the six to get ready to leave. They were grinning before he even said anything, and he saw their sea bags already stacked by the entryway. There were no secrets on a ship of war, he figured, somehow, word went around a ship faster than a pistol ball. He carefully packed his chest and wrote a note booking rooms at a pub/lodging house he knew of near to the admiralty. He would send that by messenger so it would arrive ahead of them.

The trip ashore was, to say the least, damp and Marty took a couple of rooms at the George where he and the men could dry out and stay overnight.

He sent Tom out to find a coach and horses that could carry them all to London. When he returned, he reported that he had gotten them a Park Drag and four and it would be ready to leave first thing in the morning.

Marty offered to buy them dinner in the common room, which they declined as the George's common room was officer country and they would be well out of place. They said they would get a meal in a pub down the road and promised to be on their best behaviour.

The next morning before dawn saw them loading up into the Park Drag, which looked like what it was, a former mail coach. They could get all seven of them inside at a squeeze but John Smith and Antton decided they would rather ride on top, despite it being a frosty morning.

The good thing was the ground was frozen, so they could make better time than if it were muddy, but the bad thing was the ruts were hard and the ride was comparable to a small boat in a really choppy sea. So, it was with some relief that they stopped to change horses at Petersfield and grab a pie to eat and a beer or two.

Then it was back onboard for the next leg to Guildford and an overnight stop at the Angel Posting Inn. The next morning saw them start at dawn for the run into London with a stop at Kingston for a last change of horses. They arrived at the Cromwell mid-afternoon on the eighth and settled in. The men shared two rooms, and Marty had a suite to himself.

Marty gave the boys some money and told them to get themselves some new clothes and anything else they needed. He warned them to watch out for pickpockets and not to get too drunk. He knew that letting loose sailors who had been cooped up on board ship for as long as these had was going to result in some wild behaviour, but all he could do was hope that they didn't get into too much trouble. Tom grinned and told them that he knew a good clean house where they could all have some fun with ladies of the business persuasion, which made Marty blush. He knew what he meant but wasn't quite old enough to want to explore that yet.

The next day, he visited the de Marchets family in Kensington, and they were all happy to see him again. The Count was curious as to what this 'Special Duty' was and hoped it wouldn't put Marty in harm's way. Evelyn was friendly as usual but also a little distant and he couldn't figure out why.

All too soon, he had to report at The Admiralty, and he entered the waiting room at eight o'clock in the morning to find it already crowded with officers and midshipmen looking for berths. He went to the clerk at the desk who looked down his nose at him and just said, "Yes?"

"Midshipman Stockley. I have orders to report to Admiral Hood this morning," he said.

The clerk's eyebrows went up as he looked down at his ledger and confirmed that Marty did indeed have an appointment. He called over another man and whispered something to him. He gave Marty a quick once over and left the room.

"Please wait here, you will be called when the Admiral is ready to see you," he told Marty in a marginally less superior fashion.

Marty looked around the room but there were no seats available and he was being looked at with curiosity by many of the occupants. He found a space by a wall where he could, at least, lean and waited.

A mid of around twenty years of age moved over to stand by him and introduced himself.

"Sam Granger," he said, holding his hand out. Marty shook it and replied.

"Martin Stockley."

"Are you looking for a berth?" he asked.

"No. I'm from the Falcon," Marty replied, "I have to report to Lord Hood."

"Lucky you," Sam replied, "I have been coming here for two months looking for a berth with no luck. Is the Falcon in port?" he asked hopefully.

"She's in the North on patrol," Marty told him "I helped bring a prize back to Spithead and then got orders to come here. No idea why," he said to fend off any more questions. To fill the time, he told the tale of the battle and was just running out of conversation when the desk clerk called him over.

The other man, who it transpired was a messenger, was waiting by the desk and led him out of the room. They followed several corridors and went up a couple of flights of stairs until they came to a large dark oak door that his escort knocked on and entered without waiting for a reply. Inside was a secretary's office and Marty was handed over to a man in a civilian suit with a dour look. He led him through a door at the other end of the office into a large plushily outfitted room. In the middle of the wall was a grand fireplace with a wood fire burning in it. There was a large oak desk in the middle with Admiral Lord Hood sitting behind it.

"Midshipman Stockley, milord," announced the Clerk.

Hood looked up and smiled then said, "Welcome, m'boy," and gestured to one of three chairs that were arranged in front of his desk. Marty bowed, sat on the edge of the chair where the admiral had indicated, and was just wondering who the others were for when a door on the other side of the office opened and in walked Armand Clavelle and William Wickham.

"Good, we are all here," said the Admiral.

"You know these two gentlemen, of course?" he asked Marty.

"Aye my Lord, we have met," he replied and stood to shake hands with them.

"Now Mr. Stockley, Martin, I must impress on you that everything that is said in this room cannot be repeated to anyone outside of it," said the admiral by way of introduction.

"You are entering the world of the intelligence community and your very life will depend on your ability to keep a secret. Do you give your word of honour that whatever is said here will not be divulged to another living soul?"

Marty was surprised but figured he had nothing to lose, so he said, "Aye sir, you do."

Wickham looked up and said, "The good Admiral here is one of the few senior officers in the Navy, apart from the First Naval Lord, who truly understands and supports the activities of the Intelligence Service, and we are very grateful that he has taken our advice and enabled us to try and recruit you."

What the hell!! Marty thought

Wickham continued, "You may be young, just coming up to fifteen years old, but you have developed skills that will be invaluable to the service and can be developed further over time whilst you work with us."

At least he didn't say for us, Marty thought.

The admiral interrupted, "All the time you will be 'working' with these gentlemen, your name will be on the books of a serving ship so you will not lose any sea time, and as you will undoubtedly be required to sail various vessels during this time, you will gain experience as well,"

"Quite," said Wickham, "we have need of someone who is young enough to be able to avoid suspicion, you have proven you can do that, and who can speak fluent French. Have you improved your accent?"

Marty nodded and said, "Pourquoi oui, monsieur, j'ai été en conversation avec nos membres d'équipage de Paris et Lyon."

"Oh, well done!" Armand said, "an almost perfect Parisian accent. Did you bring those six ruffians, that seem to follow you around, with you?"

"Aye, I did. They were at the Cromwell last I saw them," Marty replied.

"Good. Oh, just for the record, can you confirm that you are willing to work with us and undertake activities outside of the normal scope of Naval duties that could involve being required to go undercover into enemy territory?" said Wickham.

Marty looked at him, at Armand, and finally at the admiral, who said, "Saying no now, will not reflect on your career at all."

Marty looked back to Wickham and asked, "What do you want me to do?"

Chapter 4: A Golden Opportunity

Marty steered the fishing boat towards the French coast in a fresh South-Westerly wind and a nasty cross-chop. It was a typical French built craft not unlike the ones used by the locals in Kent. Its name was the Ariadne, which was far too grand a name for such a shabby craft. He had his crew, Tom, John, Pablo Antton, Garai, Matai, and lastly Armand, who was being noisily sick over the leeward side. He told them he was fine in ships, but little boats just made him sick.

He was aiming at the small fishing village of Wissant that was some ten miles West-Southwest of Calais. The plan was that he, Armand, Tom, Matai, and Pablo would go ashore and Antton, John, and Garai would take the boat back. They would return to pick them up in four days' time.

They were all dressed as French workmen/fishermen and would pose as a crew looking to buy a boat as theirs had been wrecked. They had forged papers with permission to travel and French money to pay for lodging. The trip was, in fact, a training run as part of the instruction the seven of them were getting since Marty's meeting in The Admiralty some three months ago. There would be another, when the three left on board would go into France and be tried.

They had been taught some interesting skills in lock picking, breaking and entering, forging (John was particularly good at that), opening and resealing documents, smuggling and concealing weapons, following unobserved, interrogation, living off the land, and concealment (taught by a man known as a Gillie from some Scottish estate). They also learned to rock climb, which was easy for them, swim (not so easy), and several ways to quietly kill someone (came naturally to all of them). They had also practiced learning cover stories and false identities. Tom and John had been taught some rudimentary French, but their language skills were not the best even with the constant help of the others.

Their mission was to go to Calais after they landed and find the offices of the Ministry of Marine. They were to observe it for two days to see who visited, when they visited, what time people started work, when it closed down, how many guards were there overnight, and what their patrol patterns were. Then they were to break in and find the office of the head man, copy his latest report to the Ministry in Paris, and leave without leaving any evidence that they had been there.

Simple.

They hit the beach at around two A.M. in the morning. The five of them jumped from the bow onto the sand and made their way inland. Armand guided them to a fisherman's cottage on the edge of the village and after a whispered exchange, they were let in. It was quite small but there was room enough for them to curl up on the floor and get a little sleep. The best that could be said about it was it was warm.

First thing the next morning, they left and headed out to the coast road that would take them to Calais. Marty suddenly had a thought; he had worked up a Parisian accent but that was totally wrong for Calais! He thought fast. How had that fisherman pronounced his words? Did he extend the vowels or shorten them?

They hit the first checkpoint, and Marty listened carefully to the way the soldiers pronounced their words and when they asked him a question, he adapted his speech to match theirs. Armand looked surprised for a second but quickly regained his composure as Marty launched into a tragic tale of how his father left him his boat, and now it was laying at the bottom of the bay all due to those damn English pigs. He even managed a heart-wrenching sob. The soldiers swallowed the story hook, line, and sinker and one even put his arm around Marty's shoulders in sympathy. They were waved through and Armand waited until they were out of hearing of the soldiers and asked, "Where did you learn to do that?"

"Do what?" said Marty.

"Mimic their accent and dialect and the act," replied Armand.

"I don't know," Marty said, "It just seemed to be the right thing to do."

Mon Dieu! We have a talent here, thought Armand.

An hour's walk saw them approaching another checkpoint and they were questioned again. These soldiers were more thorough and wanted to know why they had two Basques in their party. Marty explained that his father had found these two adrift in a mast-less boat after a huge storm five years ago and they had worked with his family ever since. He told them that they were like uncles to him now as they had looked after him since his father had died.

An officer approached, which explained the soldier's zeal. He looked the party over and asked to see in their bags. Marty opened his, revealing a dead conger eel, which he explained was a gift to the shipwright who had made their new boat. He then cursed the man because, as they didn't have enough money, he would be claiming half their catch until it was paid off. The officer recoiled from the fearsome looking beast with a curse and ordered the men to let them through.

Phew, thought Armond, *it was a good job he didn't look any closer*! Their house breaking tools and pens and papers for making copies were hidden underneath it wrapped in oilcloth.

They continued for another hour and were entering the town when they came up on another checkpoint manned by uniformed police this time. Marty went through the same routine and showed their papers, which had been marked by the previous two checkpoints. This method of monitoring people's movements was a core part of the suppression of freedom of movement brought in by the revolution.

Once again, they got through without too much difficulty. The regular practice had enabled Marty to polish his story and his accent. But to his horror, the policeman concluded that they would be returning to Wissant in their new boat, so he cancelled their return authorization.

They went down into the town through the gate and found a cheap hotel near the docks. They took just one room as that is what fishermen would do.

Their survey and observation of the office of the Ministry of Marine started the next morning. They took it in turns, in pairs, to watch the building either from a Café across the street or by loitering nearby. No pair was on observation for more than two hours, and they moved location regularly to avoid being noticed.

They identified the senior officer, who was a captain, and decided that it would be good to plot his movement and Matai was tasked with trailing him. That evening, they all got together and shared what they had seen. They had a pretty good picture of what went on during the day and what kind of people were visiting the building. Matai discovered that the captain visited a particular house four streets over from the ministry and attended a rather striking courtesan for two hours in the middle of every day. After they had eaten their evening meal, Marty and Tom went back to the ministry to see what kind of security they had overnight. They started their observations by sitting at the café and after an hour, they moved away as if they were going home, but they circled around and approached the ministry from the rear.

There were alleys running along one side and the rear of the building. Windows were set above head height, so Tom made a cup with his hands and boosted Marty up so he could look inside. He could see that the floor level of the room was higher than the pavement, so he figured there must be a cellar underneath.

The room he looked in was probably a reception room as it had high back chairs around the outside and a couple of armchairs in the middle by a low table. It was lit by several candles. There was a guard sat with his back to the window in one of the armchairs. He had a cloth tied around his neck as a napkin and was getting stuck into a selection of bread, cheeses, and sausage laid out on the table. He also had a bottle of wine and two glasses.

There was a movement at the door, and Marty ducked his head just as a second guard came in. When Marty eased his eyes over the sill, he could see that the second guard had settled into the other armchair, had placed his pistol on the table, and picked up a glass of wine.

He had seen enough and signalled Tom to lower him down. They would come back and check on the guards in an hour or so. They moved on to several other windows, and Marty noted how they were latched, what was on the inside of them, and what the room was used for.

Last, they checked the reception room again. This time, they could see that all the candles except one had been put out, and the two guards were sprawled in the armchairs fast asleep. It was just past eleven o'clock.

Once back at the room, he drew out a rough plan of what he had seen and used that to discuss a plan of action with his team. The discussion was held in French so that anyone who casually overheard their voices wouldn't be alarmed by hearing English. Probably because of his age, he always involved the team in planning, and it made the five of them work closer together.

The next day was spent in more observation and resting for they would be up most of the night.

At just after midnight, they crept out of the hotel and made their way to the Ministry. Pablo positioned himself in the shadows at the main road end of the alley that ran up the side of the building so he could keep a lookout on the front of the building. Matai set himself at the end of the alley behind the building. That left Marty, Armand, and Tom to perform the breaking and entering.

Tom boosted Marty up so he could slide a thin piece of springy metal (a Slim Jim) between the window and the frame and move it upwards to undo the latch. Once he had the window open, he quietly climbed inside and was followed by Armand. Tom stayed outside crouched down in the shadow at the base of the wall.

Together, they slipped across the room to the door, which Armand carefully opened about two inches. They listened. All they could hear was the snoring of the guards in the reception room.

They opened the door and slid out into the hallway and made their way to a staircase. Carefully, like they were walking on eggs, they tested each step-in-turn before they put their weight on it as a single creak could betray them.

They reached the landing. Marty's nerves were as taught as springs.

There was a large opulent door ahead of them. They crept up to it and listened.

All quiet.

They tried the handle.

Locked.

Marty got out a set of lockpicks and selected two that he thought would work.

It took him thirty-five seconds to open the lock.

They opened the door. It was the captain's office. Marty took out a small lantern from their bag and lit it with a flint and tinder. There was a large desk with a leather chair behind it, the top was clear of papers.

Armand went behind the desk and tried the drawers.

Locked.

He got out his lockpicks and set to work while Marty held the lantern.

It took him ten seconds to open the first and eight the second. He grinned smugly at Martin, who poked out his tongue.

They took out the papers they found inside and examined them sheet by sheet, making sure they kept them in the same order.

Armand stopped and held up one of the sheets towards the lantern and said, "Mon Dieu!"

"*What?*" said Marty.

"This letter tells that the money to pay the government, army, navy, and police for the Nord Calais region will pass through Calais on its way to Boulogne tomorrow and will be stored in the ministry overnight."

"In this building?" said Marty.

"Oui, in this building," replied Armand.

"Oh my," said Marty with a wistful look on his face, "do you think we could?"

"Mais oui, c'est possible," whispered Armand.

They copied the letter and returned all the documents to the drawers, in the same order they had come out, closed and locked them.

They left the room, locking the door behind them, and slunk back to the room they came in by. The guards were still snoring.

They opened the window and climbed out, lowering themselves down so they had a small drop to the alley. Then Tom boosted Marty back up, and he closed and locked the window.

Chapter 5: Heist The Sails

They got back to their room at around three A.M. too excited to sleep. They told the others what they had found and showed them the copy of the letter. The discussion that followed lasted to around five A.M. when they decided they should at least get a couple of hours sleep.

The next morning, Armand and Marty went to the docks to find a fishing boat. Tom stayed in the room and the two Basques went out to watch the ministry.

They found a boatyard where there were several boats similar to the Ariadne. They engaged the owner in conversation and after some fierce haggling, agreed on a price for an older boat which included a full set of sails. They pulled it around to the dock and moored it.

The next job was to provision it as if they were sailing it back to Wissant with water and some food. They didn't need anything else as all they would be doing was following the coast.

On their way back to the hotel they stopped at a leather shop and bought five large leather shoulder bags with good strong stitching.

At one A.M., the five of them stood together at the door of their room. They were all dressed in black and had black hoods to cover their faces. They looked at each other, checking that each man had everything he was supposed to, then Marty nodded and led them out.

They moved quietly, each carrying one of the leather bags, which were obviously heavy.

As they approached the Ministry, they saw that a pair of soldiers stood at the main entrance illuminated in torchlight. This was good! It would be difficult to see anything outside of the pool of light. They were also fortunate that it was cloudy, and any moonlight was faint and diffused.

Marty went first. He pulled up his hood to stop any light reflecting on his face, crossed the road well down from the Ministry, and staying close to the wall, made his way up to the alley. He checked it out up to the junction with the alley that ran along the back of the building and seeing no more soldiers and hearing no sounds of patrolling footsteps, he waited.

Tom was next and arrived quietly. He gave Marty a boost and they checked the reception room. The guards were in exactly the same position as the night before. Fast asleep.

The others arrived at regular intervals and once they were all together, they deployed as they had the night before.

They had decided to enter through the same room and Marty had it open in no time. He shimmied into the room and unwrapped a rope that he had around his waist. Armand soon joined him inside, and they hoisted up the bags one at a time using a jacket as a pad so as not to mark the windowsill. Once inside, they crept out to the door and had a quick look up and down the corridor. No one in sight and only the sound of snoring to be heard, which would cover any slight noise they made. They crept along the corridor carrying two bags each.

Armand suddenly held up his hand and they stopped. He looked at Marty and pointed to his nose. Marty looked puzzled until the unmistakable aroma of garlic wafted in from ahead.

Armand quietly put down his bags and dropped to the floor. He edged forward until he could see around the corner and then drew back.

He looked at Marty and held up one finger and then mimed sleeping.

He picked up his bags, edged forward and Marty followed. Once they got around the corner, they could see a guard propped on a chair fast asleep. More than that, there was an empty bottle beside him and a strong smell of brandy underpinning the garlic. He was dead drunk.

Talk about luck!

He was stationed outside of a door, and Armand carefully checked the handle.

No surprise, it was locked.

He got out the picks and went to work. Click! The door opened to reveal a cupboard with nothing in it except a chest.

That too was locked but fifteen seconds with the picks had it open. Inside were sacks of coins and some papers. Armand signalled to Marty to go get the fifth bag, and he slunk away as silent as a mouse to return less than a minute later.

In the meantime, Armand had been removing sacks full of sand from the leather bags. (That evening, if anybody was watching they would have seen five men on the beach filling five bags with sacks of sand which they sewed shut.) Once he had emptied a leather bag, he started transferring bags of coins into it from the chest.

The guard murmured in his sleep and shifted his position. They froze and waited until he settled. Once they were sure he was still fast asleep, they carried on. They paused after each chink of coins, afraid that they would be discovered. It was very nervous work.

Once the chest was empty, Armand filled it with the bags of sand and relocked it. While he was doing that, Marty moved the leather bags back to their entry window one at a time. They made sure they left no traces of sand on the floor then closed and relocked the door to the cupboard and carried the last two bags back. Marty put his head out of the window and whistled softly. After what seemed an age, Tom appeared below, and they started lowering the bags down to him.

They closed and re-latched the window after them, and the five quietly regrouped and headed down the alley in the opposite direction they had arrived in.

They got to the end and froze as a patrol of soldiers headed up the street past the end of the alley. Once they had past, they slipped away down to the docks. They only saw the odd drunk sleeping one off in doorways or in the filth of the gutter. After fifteen minutes, they reached the dock and boarded their new boat and stowing the bags under a pile of sail canvas.

They pulled off their hoods and just looked at each other for a long moment then, they rushed forward into a huddle, laughing as quietly as they could and patting each other on the backs.

"WHAT A THRILL!!!" Marty said in a whisper shout. "That was unbelievable!" The others all agreed but Tom shushed them and bade them calm down as the sight of a fishing boat bouncing up and down in the water might attract unwanted attention.

With an effort, they got themselves under control and changed into their fishermen's clothes. They still had to get out of the port and the best time to do that was to leave around dawn with the fishing fleet.

The sun came up at around half past eight that time of year and the fishing fleet started moving a half hour before by rowing their boats out of the harbour. To blend in and be as inconspicuous as possible, they cast off at around eight and rowed themselves out into the centre of the fleet.

It was tense. They held their breath a couple of times when guard boats passed close by manned by sleepy sailors of the French Navy, but they made it out and as soon as they could they raised sail and headed down the coast South to Wissant.

They had been on French soil for four days.

The trip down the coast didn't take long, and they arrived before midday. They had discussed what they would do with the boat and as it had nothing to distinguish it from any other boat, they decided to make a gift of it to their ally who had sheltered them that first night.

The Ariadne wasn't due to pick them up until dusk, so they had to hide out for the rest of the day until their pickup at around eight P.M. They went back to the house they stayed at before and gave their friend (they were never given his name) the good news that he was now the owner of a used but serviceable fishing boat. He was overjoyed and made them a meal of a wonderful fish stew.

They knew the army would move the chest today and they were praying that no one had opened it and discovered the theft. So, Antton went out and found a concealed spot where he could see the road and watched. Around two P.M., he came back and said a squad of soldiers escorting a wagon had passed heading South. It looked like the deception was working so far but once the chest reached Boulogne, the game would be up.

Dusk came, and they were waiting on the beach as the Ariadne slid up on the sand. They boarded and headed home with a great sense of relief. All they had to do now was avoid the English blockade.

Chapter 6: The S.O.F

They were enjoying an enforced rest due to a huge storm that was lashing the channel with winds that were almost due East, trapping all shipping on the East coast in port. They were at their training base in Kent, which was a manor house outside of Deal, when they heard a carriage pull up outside and then the front door bang.

Marty got up to see who it was when the door opened and in walked William Wickham and Admiral Lord Hood. All the men rose to their feet but were told to relax and sit down. The steward, Will, came and took their coats and hats, Hood whispered something to him. The Admiral made his way over to the fire and raised his coat tails with his back to the flames to warm his behind.

"Filthy weather," he said.

Wickham stole the chair Marty had been sitting in, prompting Tom to offer his, but Marty waved him back to it and went and sat on the arm of the chair Armand was in.

"Well, I must say you gentlemen have stirred up a hornet's nest over the other side of the Channel," Wickham said, "the French are totally bemused as to when and where their money was stolen, and they are bringing in a special team from Paris to investigate. We expect heads to roll – literally. They have brought in more soldiers, checkpoints have been doubled, all movement stopped. They have even beached the fishing fleets."

"The loss of funds hurts them as well," chipped in the Admiral, "they can't afford to lose money like that and as a consequence, all their local civil servants, police, Military, and Navy won't get paid." He paused as he took a glass of Brandy from Will who had returned from the kitchen with a tray full of drinks.

"The Admiralty and the government have been at loggerheads over what to do with the gold. But in the end, they decided that the money should be kept in the project in the main part," he continued after a large gulp of the amber liquid. He liked to think of this whole adventure as his project. "The crown will take an eighth, you gentlemen," he indicated the six with a sweep of his hand, "will share an eighth," grins all around, "your officers, an eighth, and your admiral will get his eighth," he beamed at them in a benevolent way. "The other half will go into funding operations. Your unexpected success has prompted the First Naval Lord to make you into a Special Unit. Part of the Navy but separate from it."

"Talking of which, what we have in mind is that we want this group to have two functions," Wickham said.

"First is to infiltrate into French held territory and liaise with local agents, help them with specific missions, and provide a means to get them into and out of their operational areas," he looked around the room to see how that went down, "and the second is to take on operations the regular Navy are not able to do, or do not want to take on because they are too specialized or they consider them 'dishonourable'."

"In other words, you do the Navy's dirty work." Hood smiled wolfishly, then added, "Work that should be quite profitable! You will have some Marines added to your team who have been chosen because they have particular skills. Armand! You have been made lieutenant based on your previous rank in the Royal French Navy and will be in overall command. Martin, despite his age, will be second in command. You are required to make a list of equipment and vessels that you will need."

"Gentlemen, a toast!" said the admiral, "To the 'Special Operations Flotilla.' May you cause confusion and consternation to the enemy!"

They raised their glasses and drained them to heel taps and cried, "Confusion and Consternation."

The meeting broke up and Armand and Marty were given written orders which officially made them part of the S.O.F.. Their orders also made it abundantly clear that outside of the flotilla, they were to present themselves as a training unit and that the mere existence of a Special Unit was the highest of secrets.

They were joined by their Marines a week later, and a strange collection of individuals they were too. There were a couple of ex-poachers who were excellent woodsmen and sharpshooters. Another couple who were self-confessed former burglars. A former blacksmith, an ex-locksmith, an engineer, and a livery man. A truly eclectic collection but with the common traits of intelligence and initiative. They were surprised to be under the command of a Frenchman and a fifteen-year-old midshipman who apparently, already had a reputation as a ruthless killer. As was typical of the Marines, they accepted their fate stoically and reserved judgment until shown one way or another.

They all settled into the house in their own way. The Marines preferred a barracks style set up and Armand and Marty were happy to let them. Joint training was more an exchange of skills than a formal training session, and all benefited.

Their first task was to set up a system whereby agents could be delivered to the French coast and the information they gathered could be easily brought back. They would also need to be able to recover agents from France and return them to England. So, in their own style they got everybody together, presented the problem, and invited everyone to make suggestions.

They had sourced a very large blackboard that would make a schoolmaster weep with envy, and Marty wrote down every suggestion as they were put forward. One suggestion was to disguise the agents as logs and float them ashore, another to find a bay, miles away from anywhere, and drop them there - both had their limitations.

Then someone mentioned that the local smugglers were running back and forth to France all the time and could run right into the ports without being questioned.

This was much more interesting.

They homed in on that and started working out how they could use it. First, they thought they could set up their own smuggling racket but that would be difficult as the contacts on both sides were extremely wary of new faces.

Then Fred Billings, one of the Marines, said, "Why don't we just take over one of the local gangs?" Arnaud stared at the ceiling as he thought that over, and Marty looked out of the window deep in thought. The men looked at each other and waited.

"C'est bonne," said Armand.

"Perfect," smiled Marty, "which gang is well established but not so big that we will have too much trouble muscling in on it?"

Nobody knew, although there were a few suggestions from John Smith, who came from that part of Kent originally.

"John, you obviously know the local area. Why don't you go and see what you can find out." Armond said. "Corporal Hythe can go with you as backup. Take some money for bribes but don't flash it around too much or someone will hit you on the head for it."

"Tom, take two men and set up a watch on the beach at Deal. See what boats go out and when. Try and identify the skippers and where they get together. We will need to make it clear to all of them we are now in charge and the easiest way to do that is come down hard in front of as many of them as we can," Marty added.

Afterwards, Marty and Armand sat together over a glass of wine and talked over their chances of success.

"You know what we are going to do will be totally illegal," said Marty. "If it goes wrong, we could all get hung."

"Ahh, but if it works, we will 'ave an invaluable resource for the intelligence service," replied Armand. "It will be worth the risk."

"Well, we better make a very fast and firm impression on the smugglers and show them we can make life even better in return or we won't stay in charge for long," said Marty feeling nervous in spite of Armand's confidence.

"Oh, I am sure you can manage that," laughed Armand.

After several weeks of surveillance and careful intelligence gathering by John Smith, they had their target. It was a local gang run by two brothers who had half a dozen boats. They specialised in running brandy and wine from France to England and paid in gold and silver. They had a network of outlets for their goods that reached all the way to London, which was also useful. They had found out that there was a get together planned to celebrate one of their skipper's birthdays at a local pub and all the gang would be there.

They armed themselves well with pistols, knives, cutlasses, and clubs. Marty had his weapons harness under a long, loose coat and had both his pepper pot pistols, his fighting knife, and his hanger. Armand had stilettos in both of his boots, throwing knives in sleeve sheaths, and a pair of pistols as well as a sword. There were fourteen of them and around thirty smugglers. They reckoned they had them out numbered.

The approach to the pub was crucial. They didn't want to be seen and have someone give the game away. So, stealth was the first order. Marty and six men went to the rear of the pub, climbing through the gardens of the houses next to it to get there. Armand with the rest of the men were going in the front door.

Marty and his men waited and listened, there was the bang of a door opening and a pistol shot. Marty wrenched open the door and with pistol in his hand, led the men in through the kitchen to the common room.

The first thing he saw was Armand standing with his men fanned out behind him facing the smugglers, who had drawn weapons. He fired his pistol into the ceiling and immediately cranked the next barrel of the Nock into the firing position. The arrival of the second group stopped the smugglers mid-step as they surged toward Armand and his men, and the multiple clicks of pistols being cocked absolutely got their attention.

"What be the meaning of this?" said a man who they had identified as the enforcer of the gang. A violent, sadistic bastard who was more feared than respected called Sam Brown. The word was he had beaten to death a prostitute not three days before.

"We are here to make you an offer you can't refuse," Marty said.

"And what be that, boy?" said the man.

"You work for us from now on and we make yer rich," said Marty.

"Work for you, boy? You aint got the balls to take what be ours," he said and started to pull out a knife.

Marty didn't hesitate. His left hand went behind him and came forward in a smooth, well-practiced action. Sam Brown looked surprised as the fighting knife sank cleanly into his throat and he folded to the floor, dead before he landed. There was a collective gasp from the room as much from the casual violence meted out as the fact that a fresh-faced teenager had delivered it.

"Anybody else got something to say?" Marty asked as he stepped up and pushed him onto his back with his foot so he could recover his knife.

There was silence, then a man they knew to be the boss said, "I think you made yer point and you have my attention, so what be yer offer?"

Arnaud stepped forward and said, "Let us sit and we will explain. There is a back room, no? Monsieur Clarence?"

Clarence looked surprised at the French accent but nodded to a door to the right of where Marty had entered.

"My lieutenants?" he asked, indicating a younger man that looked like him and a second that was obviously his brother.

"Yes, your son and your brother can join as well," Arnaud said.

They left the room in the charge of their men under Tom, and the five of them went to talk. On the way, Marty indicated to the barkeep that he should bring drinks. The room was small, had a square table and six chairs. The smugglers sat on the far side against the wall, and Marty and Armand sat opposite with their backs to the door.

"Yer seem to know all about us, but we don't know anything about you," Clarence said, "So, why don't you introduce yerself."

"My name is Armand, and this is my compatriot Martin. We represent a well-connected consortium of individuals who are, shall we say, tolerant of your commercial activities, but who would like to use them to forward their own interests."

"We can guarantee you immunity from the excise service and can help you expand your activities," added Marty.

"Sounds like a reasonable offer if its genuine, so why didn't you just come to me with it without all this . . ." he waved a hand at the door.

"Would you have listened? Or just cut our throats?" Marty asked.

"Point taken," Clarence conceded with a thoughtful frown. "Alright, let's talk on this and see where it goes."

"But Pa, they killed Sam!" cried his son, Jonathan.

"I were probably gonna kill him meself seein' as he beat poor Molly to death. She only held back a shillin' to pay for her boy to see the doctor an didn't deserve that, so shut up an' listen."

"Here be our offer," said Marty, "we provide protection from the excise and ease you into new markets for the goods. We also provide funds to enable you to bring more goods back in. In return, you help us with our interests by smuggling goods and people into France and occasionally bringing special packages and people back."

"For which you will be paid handsomely," added Armand, who sat back in his chair with his arms crossed.

"I know you now," Clarence said after looking closely at the two of them, "I seen you at the big house, and I seen who visited you. What's to stop me telling the magistrate that Navy men be trying to muscle in to the smugglin' trade?"

Marty dropped back into full dialect as he pulled one of his pistols and cocked it, "Fer one thing, you be dead as soon as you did." He pointed it straight between Clarence's eyes, "or I could drop yer righ' now and take over anyway. Or," he lowered the hammer and replaced the gun in its holster and went back to his 'Navy' voice, "you can make some money, grow your business, and do your country a service. Your choice."

Armand laughed. "My young friend can be very direct but 'e does get to the heart of the matter. In the end, we make you an offer that is a win for both of us. Do we have an accord?"

Clarence thought for a long moment, his eyes shifting from Armand to Marty and back. Then, he looked at his brother and son. His brother shrugged, and his son nodded. Finally, he nodded and held out his hand, which Armond shook first and then Marty. Peter followed suit. He looked at his son and said, "Jonathan, shake the men's hands." His son hesitated and looked as if he would rather grab a snake, but then he looked at Marty, who just grinned at him and said,

"Come on mate, it will be fun and you aint really going to miss that asshole, are you?" and held out his hand. Jonathan looked back at him and recognised that inside the steely killer was a teenager just like him and shook his hand.

"Now, if we can get some paper, pen, and ink, we can write up a partnership agreement. You can read?" said Armand.

"Aye, I can. So don' try to add nothin' we aint already agreed."

"Wouldn't dream of it, mon amie," said Armand in his most urbane voice.

"Now, let's 'ave a drink and you can tell me what's a Frenchie doing working for the government," said Clarence.

"I'll give the news to the good people out there," said Marty, "I bet it's pretty tense, and we don't want to get off to a bad start." Bill barked a short laugh at that, thinking ironically of his dead henchman.

Once back at the house, they sent a message to Wickham telling him they had established a way to get agents and messages to and from France. They also told him they wanted a Cutter and a dozen extra men to man it. Just normal top men and wasters, no special skills needed but men that could be trusted.

They decided they would moor the Cutter at Richborough, which was an hour's ride up the coast, and they started to look for a new headquarters nearer to there. Deal was alright but with only a beach and no harbour it had limited benefits.

What they needed was a building that could act as a shore base, training ground, and store that was close to the harbour and had easy access to the road to Deal. They eventually found a farmhouse with ample outbuildings not far from the river and remote enough to ensure privacy. It was empty as the previous tenant had been evicted, and they moved in immediately.

Chapter 7: Smuggling (And Other Services)

"What we need," said Armand, "is a ship that the Sans-Culottes will think is one of theirs."

"What, like the Fortune? French built and can be flagged either way?" Marty replied.

"Exactement," Armand nodded.

"Why?" Marty asked.

"I 'ave an idea 'ow to disrupt the trade between America and France," he replied, "They will not appreciate being robbed by French Privateers."

"Why don't we get the boys out of Deal to look for a likely candidate and then figure out how to acquire it," offered Marty, "I'm going over there tonight as we are taking our first agent over so I can ask them. I can also have a look into Boulogne and see if there is anything interesting there."

"OK, but nothing too big, Oui?" said Armand.

That evening, Marty took one of the horses they kept for just this purpose and rode to Deal. He had only recently learned how to ride and still didn't feel completely at home in the saddle, but at least he didn't get such a sore arse and thighs as he did when he started.

When he got there, he went to the Waggon and Horses. Bill Clarence and his brother Peter sat at a table with a third man who he knew as Ash, one of the skippers. He joined them at the table.

"Evenin' Marty," said Bill, "yer package arrived at the Kings Arms this afternoon. A bookish looking fellow, nuttin' to look at."

"Perfect for the work then," said Marty, "I was wondering, have you seen any French ships around the size of a sloop laid up in any of the ports over there that we could acquire?"

"What you want one of them fer?" asked Peter.

"Well, there be a lot of 'neutral' ships supplying goods to the French and we figure that if'n we could divert some of those goods over to here and put the blame on French privateers it would be good for business."

Ash and Bill laughed at that and Bill said, "The perfect crime and who would man this ship?"

"Why, we figured that for a cut of the take, your men might like to make up the numbers," Marty said with a smirk.

"You mean we make up a crew like a privateer?" Bill asked.

"Yes, top heavy on men so we can man more than one prize per voyage. Get up close and board them in French waters, either offload their cargo to our ship and let them sail on empty or take them as a prize and put the crew in a long boat so they can row ashore," Marty explained.

"If we bring any boats back, they will have to be 'cleaned' before we sell them on. So, it may be better to sink them if they be obviously foreign built."

"Well, you gentlemen will have to think on that fer later," said Ash, "It be time to get under way."

"I'll see you on the beach by the 'Carine'," said Marty and got up to go to the Kings Arms.

'The package' sat in the common room and looked exactly as Bill had described. Marty checked the room for any threats, then made his way to the table and pulled up a chair.

"Good Evening, is the weather in London fine?" He asked.

"No, the snow has been heavy," was the reply. *Recognition signal requested and given,* thought Marty.

"Come, your transport awaits," said Marty. He waited for the man to stand and retrieve his bag then turned and walked to the door.

He looked up and down the street, took the man by the arm, and led him to the beach. It was quiet. Word had gotten around that something was 'on' that evening and the locals had prudently stayed indoors. Once there, he found the fishing boat that was pulled up on the sand with Carine on the stern.

Ash stuck his head over the rail and said, "Get aboard. The horses are on their way."

There was a set of steps to one side, and they climbed up and on to the boat. Just then, two draft horses in harness came down the beach driven by a single man accompanied by five fishermen. Marty watched with professional interest as the men hitched the horses to two tackles that were laid out from the bow. The horses took the strain and the boat started to slip down the sand. Marty saw it was aided by pieces of wood laid at regular intervals for the keel to run over. The boat slid into the surf and the men boarded over the sides.

When the horses were chest deep, the tackles were cast off and they rowed out past the surf until they could raise the sail and make way. They were heading for Calais on a regular run.

"Has it quietened down over there now?" asked Marty once they were settled on course.

"Yes, it has, but it were right awkward for a bit." He looked at Marty suspiciously. "What do you know about that?" he asked.

"Oh, I just heard that they lost some money is all," Marty replied with what could only be described as a feral grin.

"Hmm, well it be said they lost a great deal of money," said Ash, "and whoever took it got clean away."

"It was probably the best heist in recent history," said their passenger. "It caused absolute chaos throughout the Ministry of Marine and a major witch hunt. The civil servants, Army, and Navy didn't get paid that quarter."

"Yeah, the cost of bribes went through the roof because of it. They had to make up the money from somewhere," moaned Ash.

"And several high-ranking soldiers lost their heads over it as well," the passenger concluded.

Marty sat back and just smiled. The eighth he had shared with Armand had almost equalled the prize money from the Mediterranean and was earning nice interest in the four percent.

It was a dull, overcast night and the trip across only took a couple of hours. As they approached the dock, it was just after eleven P.M. The passenger changed into fisherman's clothes and after they had talked with the clerk of the docks and paid the usual graft, he accompanied Marty and Ash to visit the merchant who was supplying their goods. As they passed an alley where the torch at the entrance had 'conveniently' gone out, he slid away from them into the shadows.

When they entered the warehouse, they were met by a merchant who Ash had obviously done business with before. He looked suspiciously at Marty as Ash introduced him as their new business partner.

Marty said in French, "*Good evening, sir. It is my pleasure to make your acquaintance. I would like to discuss the purchase of some of your best brandy and a selection of Claret and Bordeaux wines.*"

Ash looked at him with his mouth agape and eyes wide. The merchant was taken aback by the young man with the Parisienne accent and hesitated for a second before replying.

"*But yes sir, and how will you be paying?*"

"*In Louis D'Or, naturally,*" said Marty and flourished a coin he had concealed in his hand. The merchant took it, bit it, then went to a table where there were some scales and weighed it. He nodded and went to put it in his pocket.

Marty's fighting knife made an uncomfortably loud thud as the point drove into the table one inch from his hand.

"*Tsk tsk sir, we must finalize our business before you get to keep that trinket,*" Marty said with a smile that made the merchant's blood run cold. "*I would like to sample what you have on offer and then we can get down to business.*"

The man practically ran to some casks and dipped a couple of glasses of amber brandy using a cup on the end of a long thin handle and offered them to Ash and Marty. He was wringing his hands as the glasses were rolled in their hands to warm them, the brandy sniffed and finally tasted.

"Better stuff than we is normally getting," said Ash.

"Yes, it's not bad is it," replied Marty and to the merchant, *"excellent we will take 10 casks."* Each cask held four and a half gallons or twenty litres and would have been classified as pins in England.

They sampled Claret and Bordeaux wines and selected the ones they wanted.

The merchant had their order loaded into a couple of carts and added up the bill, which he itemised and handed to Marty.

Marty made a show of looking at it and said, *"I believe you made a mistake."*

The merchant, who still had a very clear image in his mind of the huge knife appearing out of nowhere, gulped and took the paper back and examined it.

"Oh, mon Dieu, I forgot your discount of ten," he looked at Marty, who just examined his fingernails, *"No, fifteen percent."*

Marty relented, smiled, and said, *"Perfect! It has been a joy doing business with you and I look forward to returning and doing much more."* That mollified the merchant somewhat, and when Marty counted out a pile of Louis d'Or coins in payment, he forgot about feeling put out altogether.

They rode the carts back to the boat as that way an onlooker would probably not notice they were a man short.

When they got to the dock, Marty and Ash went directly below and checked the receipt the merchant had given them. The crew, aided by the merchant's men, loaded their cargo into the hold and covered it with fishing nets.

"Why did you push him so hard on the discount?" Ash asked, "We had plenty of profit margin without it."

"It was Armand's suggestion," Marty replied, "The merchant will remember me as a sharp businessman and one who is ruthless. The Louis d'Or coins were there to fix in his mind that we are serious and have good connections. He doesn't realise they were nicked from them in the first place."

"You mean the theft the passenger mentioned?" Ash asked in some awe.

Marty just smiled then the mate came in with the tally of what had been loaded.

The whole exercise from landing to being ready to leave had taken less than three hours and they were able to leave the Harbour at two in the morning just at the turn of the tide.

Marty stood on deck as they left and had a good look at the ships lying in the harbour. He couldn't see much, but nothing stood out as a likely candidate for their second ship.

As they approached the beach, they hoisted two lights, a red over a white, and they were answered with a white over a red. The all clear. They dropped the sails one hundred yards offshore, and rowed the last stretch through the surf. The horses were waiting. The crew turned the boat so she was stern first and as soon as it was shallow enough, four of them jumped over the side into the water to steady her. The horses were hitched, and the boat pulled ashore.

It was what happened next that impressed Marty. Around thirty men appeared out of the dark and formed a line from the boat to the firm land behind the sandy beach. The crew handed out the cargo piece by piece and it was passed rapidly up the line to waiting carts. They were completely unloaded in less than fifteen minutes and everyone was on their way home. It was a slick well organised exercise and he now knew why it was so difficult for the excise to catch the smugglers at it without knowing when the boats were arriving.

He stayed what was left of the night at the Wagon and Horses and made his way back to their Headquarters after a hearty breakfast.

When he got there, it was all quiet and no one seemed to be around, so he stabled his horse and went into the house. The only person there was their steward, Will Barbour, who told him that the Cutter had arrived, and everyone had gone down to the harbour to check it over. He changed into his uniform and walked over there.

When he got there, he found that it had been sailed in by the extra crew they had asked for under the command of a Bosun's mate. To his utter surprise he saw the unmistakable figure of Wilson, the giant of a man that he had sailed with on the Fortune and recognised du Demaine as well. The cutter, called the Snipe, was tied up to the wharf next to the Ariadne so he walked up the gangway.

Armand was dressed in uniform and was just setting up to read himself in when he saw Marty walk up the gangplank. He waited until he had made his way over, welcomed him, and asked,

"Did it go well?"

"Yes, just as expected," was the reply.

He then stood erect and taking a deep breath, began to read himself in. The orders were loose and basically said they were an independent unit and could do whatever they liked. All in all, it was a formality to make the men comfortable, but they had their first ship.

Marty made his way around the deck greeting the new men and trying to learn their names. He soon found Wilson and du Demaine, greeted them by name, and said,

"I am very pleased to see you both, but how on earth did you get yourselves on this detail?"

Wilson stepped forward and said,

"Well you see, sir, the Fortune were brought back into Portsmouth fer a minor refit when this Lieutenant came on board and spoke to Mr. Gentry. He called fer us to go to his cabin like and we was asked if we would be interested in joining you as crew on a Cutter. He said that you were there with the rest of the men from the Fortune and had mentioned our names. He said he had orders from Admiral Hood."

"Ahh," said Marty, "that old fox doesn't miss a trick. I bet he read your names in the report of the taking of those prizes in the Mediterranean."

He turned to du Demaine and said in French, "*Hello Roland. We will need your knowledge for the work we do here,*" and then in English, "Did they tell you anything about what we do?"

"Nary a word," said Wilson, "But the boys have mentioned that it's not what it seems and to expect a few surprises."

Marty went to Armand and said, "We better brief these men on security and what we are doing. I'm sure that they are all dedicated Navy, so they won't run, but they need to know to keep their traps shut and the best place to do that is at sea where no one can overhear."

"Agreed," said Armand, "let's get under sail."

The good thing about cutters is they have sweeps, oars that can be used if needed for manoeuvring. They cast off and using the sweeps and the sluggish current of the river Stour, they made their way out of the estuary and to sea.

They sailed South through Sandwich Bay towards Deal and once they were off Deal Beach, Marty called all the men to assemble on deck.

"You new men have all been hand-picked by the admiralty as being true Navy men who are loyal to the crown and the service, and who can be trusted. You are probably wondering what the hell you have gotten yourselves into," said Marty in a voice loud enough to carry to the bowsprit.

"I am sure that all of you have been given hints by the old hands to expect the unexpected or things not being what they seem. Well, I can tell you that to the outside world we are a training unit and if anybody asks, that is all you tell them. But to the admiralty and the Intelligence Service of his Majesty's Government, we are the Special Operations Flotilla, or the S.O.F. as we call it, and answer directly to the First Naval Lord and Admiral Hood. If you tell anybody outside of this crew anything about what you do or have done as part of the S.O.F., you will be hung for treason.

You will get extra pay for hazardous duty, be paid in cash, and will all benefit from higher rates of prize money than normal sailors." He paused and looked around at the men who looked surprised at that and more than a few were grinning.

"Discipline will be more relaxed than you are used to, and you will understand why with time. But that doesn't mean you can take the piss! If we don't get what we expect from you, life will get very unpleasant very quickly. If any of you doubt my word on this, talk to the men who have sailed with me in the past. Any questions?"

One man raised his hand,

"Do you mean we don't get paid with chits?"

"Yes, you get paid with cold, hard coin."

There was a general murmur around the men then another hand went up.

"It's all well getting paid in coin but if we's not allowed ashore to spend it what's the point?"

"You will spend more time ashore with us than you ever have. You will understand why later as well. But that doesn't mean you can go off and visit your people in Portsmouth or wherever. You will be restricted to Deal while you are here. There are plenty of whores there and most of them are clean."

That caused a laugh.

"But be warned. Run, and we will hunt you down like a dog and hang you ourselves or cut your throat and bury you in a ditch. We look after our own and if anyone betrays us, then God help them. Anyone want to leave now? He indicated the side and the waves lapping gently passed them. No one moved or said anything. There was not even a murmur.

"So, you are all in?"

"AYE AYE, SIR!" was the reply.

Chapter 8: A Cutting Trip

Marty was in the Wagon and Horses meeting with Bill Clarence, the leader of the smugglers.

"So, there is a Corvette laid up in St. Valery up the Somme River," said Marty.

"That's what we saw," Bill replied, "and when we asked, they said she 'ad been brought in as she 'ad lost a mast and while they were fixing 'er the army came and took all their gunners. Then the rest of her crew were dispatched to Brest to a new frigate. She's only got an 'arbour crew on board now."

"Sounds ideal," said Marty.

Just then, an argument broke out between a couple of the S.O.F. and some smugglers. Marty watched as it progressed from loud voices to pushing, and the first punch being thrown. It soon collapsed into a general melee and as long as no weapons were pulled, he and Bill were happy to let it run its course.

"Well, I'll get back and start working out a plan with Armand," he said, "but have your men ready to sail at short notice. We will need at least forty to get her back here."

On his way out, he ducked a stray punch and pushed the fighter back into the fray. He then tossed a couple of coins to the landlord and told him "drinks all round."

Later, he sat with Armand poring over a map of the French coast and particularly the area around the estuary of the river Somme. It was tricky to navigate with anything bigger than a fishing boat as there was a single deep channel that ran from the sea up to the village of St. Valery. For the skipper of the Corvette to make the entrance, he must have been desperate and unable to get to Boulogne or Le Touquet, which had more accessible harbours.

"We will need forty men to sail her out and that is a lot to get on one cutter, isn't it?" asked Armand.

"It is, and we will need at least 10 men to sail the cutter home, meaning we will need fifty men plus you me and the Bosun."

"Can we use some of the smuggler's boats?" asked Armand.

"No, they don't want to spoil their relationship with the locals," replied Marty.

"So, we're left with just the Ariadne and the Snipe. We can get 'ow many on the Snipe?"

"Well, she normally has a crew of twenty and the trip to St. Valery will take at least ten hours including navigating the river, if we have a favourable wind. I wouldn't want to cram more than forty on her. We could get another ten on the Ariadne if we tow her back unmanned."

"So, I command the Snipe and you command the Ariadne on the way down, and on the way back you command the Corvette as you have sailed one before and tow the Ariadne," said Armand.

"That sounds like a plan," said Marty.

"What time of day would you want to cut it out?"

"If we want to navigate the deep channel, then somewhere around mid-day at high tide which means arriving at the estuary around ten in the morning," replied Armand.

"Then we had better leave here on the evening tide to give us some leeway in case of contrary weather. When do we cast off?" Marty asked.

"When is the full moon?" asked Armand.

Marty consulted an almanac and said, "Eighteenth and nineteenth."

"Then we leave on the seventeenth to make sure that if we have to navigate the Somme at night, we can see what where we are going," concluded Armand.

"Good, that gives us five days to prepare. I'll get started first thing in the morning," said Marty.

The next five days saw busy but not frenetic activity as the Snipe and the Ariadne were provisioned and prepared. They checked every inch of cordage on both vessels, re-blacking it and fitted new gaskets where needed. The guns on the Snipe were overhauled but the twelve six-pounders didn't pack much of punch. Marty had plans to replace them with twenty-four-pound carronades. He just had to convince Armand that it was a good idea. They made sure the sweeps were in good condition and they had spares as they would be needed to get them up the Somme if the wind wasn't favourable.

He took time to visit Bill at the Wagon and Horses and briefed him on the trip. The forty men would be at the dock on time and be fully equipped. Marty thanked him and said that he hoped to get the Corvette without a fight, but it was best to be prepared. As he left, Bill couldn't help thinking what made a sixteen-year-old miner's son from Dorset into the confident, young man he saw walking out of the pub. There was no swagger, just a cool confidence in his ability to handle anything that the world threw at him, and then, of course, there was that big bastard of a knife he had tucked under his jacket in the small of his back.

On his way to the stables, Marty found his way blocked by Susie, the Innkeepers daughter. She was a pretty seventeen-year-old buxom brunette who was on the prowl for a husband and, like most young girls of the time, she was more than prepared to get her chosen man by seduction. She wore a low-cut dress that showed off her ample bosom to good advantage, and she had a way of swishing her hips that encouraged lewd thoughts.

"Hello Martin," she purred, "where be you off to?"

"If I told you that," he said with a smile, "I would have to kill you."

"Well, we wouldn't want that now would we. I wouldn't be anywhere near as much fun dead, now would I?" She replied and leaned back against the wall, inviting him to move in on her.

Marty was sorely tempted, but her timing was all wrong, he had to get back to The Farm. So, he leaned forward, kissed her soundly on the lips, pulled her away from the wall, turned her towards the entrance to the Inn, and slapped her on the behind.

"I have to go," he said, "maybe next time."

She flounced and looked back at him over her shoulder. "If there is a next time, sailor boy," she taunted.

He got his horse and led it out of the stable, having to adjust himself to make it comfortable to mount. He knew all about the relations between men and women and what went on. He was now at an age where he was having the urge to try it for himself but right now, he had to focus on the job in hand. Life was difficult sometimes.

Back at the farm, everything seemed to have gone as planned. Both the cutter and fishing boat were ready to go with food and water being loaded at the last minute. Marty carefully checked the stores to make sure no one had sneaked any alcohol onboard. He wanted strict control of any that they were given, as even the best sailors tended to binge if it were freely available.

Nine o'clock saw the dock full of men bristling with weapons. Marty called off the ten crew for the Ariadne, which included both Tom and John Smith, and got them boarded. Five was enough to sail the boat, so he split his four regular Navy men and teamed them with three smugglers per watch. The Ariadne was almost identical to the boats they used so they knew how to sail her. This would also keep the men fresh doing four hours on and four off.

Armand soon had the cutter ready to go and was casting off. Marty waited until she was out into the stream and then cast off the Ariadne and fell in a cable length astern of her.

The weather was seasonal, and the conditions were fine as they stood out into the Dover Straights and turned due South with the wind on their beam.

They were not particularly fast craft and given the conditions were able to log eight to ten knots. Although it was fine sailing weather to start with, it all changed around midnight. The wind started to veer from the West round towards the South and the sea started to pick up. They were forced to tack to make any Southing at all. If they had been in pure square riggers, they would have been in even more trouble, but the gaff rigged sails both vessels had allowed them to sail close to the wind.

It took a further nine hours to travel the last thirty-five miles to see them off the Somme Estuary. They reduced sail and started to feel their way in. The Snipe had men swinging a lead to take the depth as they crept along under minimum sail even though they had smugglers aboard who had entered the river before.

The wind suddenly dropped to practically nothing, so they ran out the sweeps and flew the French flag to confuse any observers. Having no sail set helped but anyone who knew their ships would spot that the Snipe had a British rig. The channel turned to the Southwest, and they continued on for a couple of miles. The village with its quay came into view and there, tied up, was the Corvette just as had been reported.

Marty could see she probably carried eighteen guns in ports along the sides and at a guess four pop guns on each of the fore and aft decks. She looked deserted with her sails in harbour gaskets and her yards all askew as if she had been abandoned. The distance dropped until the Snipe passed the Corvette and turned to moor with her bow pointing down river directly behind her. By now, they were beginning to attract attention, so Armand started shouting orders in French, and the men ran around as if they understood them.

Marty ran the Ariadne up alongside the Corvette, and one of his men hooked onto her chains with a boathook. He scrambled up the side followed by all the men. He also shouted orders in French for effect, but his men knew what they had to do without them. Half went below to look for the harbour crew. A couple of minutes later, there was a very womanly squeal from the captain's cabin. He was tempted to go and see what was afoot but at that moment the men from the Snipe arrived. He now had his crew.

He detailed Tom and John Smith to get the harbour gaskets off her and to set her up for sailing. He looked over the side to the quay. Armand was there and called up in French, *"Get her moving as fast as you can, we will follow you out"*

"Oui, mon Capitaine," called Marty back to him.

"Get a leadsman in the chains," he ordered, "and break out the sweeps, we're going to have to row the bitch out of here."

He suddenly realized Bill Clarence was standing beside him.

"Didn't know you were coming on this pleasure cruise," he grinned at him.

"Wouldn't miss it for the world," Bill laughed back.

Marty noticed a movement on the Quay. He looked over and saw a local with a startled look suddenly turn and run towards the town.

Damn he must have heard us speak in English! Marty drew a pistol, but the man was too far away to drop.

"Damn," he swore, "Get those sweeps out and get us away NOW!" he shouted, "we've been rumbled!"

He looked to the guns and saw that only four per side were there.

"Get those guns loaded with canister," he yelled at Tom, who grabbed two hands and went down below to find the magazine. He was back two minutes later empty handed.

"Not a grain of powder on board, sir,'" he reported.

"Shit." Marty thought hard.

"Get all the men to prime their pistols and lay them down along the Larboard side of the deck and then get them back to getting us out of here."

"John! Get the Ariadne tied up astern for towing."

"Bill, put two men on each sweep and run out as soon as we be clear."

"Cut the moorings!"

The thud of axes was soon replaced by a swoosh as the mooring ropes dropped over the side and the men pushed her away from the quay. The current was sluggish, so she moved slowly.

There was a shout from the direction of the town and a half dozen blue uniforms appeared a hundred yards away. One knelt and there was a puff of smoke and a bang as he fired his musket.

A voice to his right said, "May I, sir?" and he saw that it was one of his marines, Dibble, if he remembered correctly, an ex-poacher and crack shot.

"Be my guest," said Marty.

Dibble cocked his musket and rested it on the rail as he took aim. He became still, took a breath, and let it out. The hammer flipped forward, the primer lit with a whoosh, then the main charge went off with a bang and a cloud of smoke. One hundred yards away, one of the blue uniforms jerked and fell to the ground. There was a second shot, and Marty saw that another marine had fired as well. He didn't see if he had hit.

He went to the wheel and took over the helm. The men were now working the sweeps in a steady rhythm set by Bill, who was manning one of the sweeps himself. He looked behind and the Snipe was just pushing away from the dock. The blue uniforms had disappeared.

They were out in the centre of the channel when a lookout spotted horsemen on the South bank. They were keeping pace with them when one turned away and galloped off.

They turned to the Northwest and were moving a little faster, Marty ordered the men on the sweeps to be changed.

"Deck there," hailed a lookout, "there be something 'appening on that headland up ahead."

Marty handed over the wheel to Tom and grabbing a telescope, headed up the main mast shrouds to the topsail yard. He steadied the glass and focused on the point. He was a little confused by what he saw at first. he could see cavalry, but they were leading their horses away on foot. Then he swung back to the point, and his breath caught in his throat. Horse artillery! There were three Howitzers lined up on the point and he was the target.

He shinned down a stay to the deck and ran to the stern rail, waved at the Snipe, which was forty yards behind and yelled. Armand appeared at the bow. Marty pointed to the headland and mimed shooting. Armand looked confused then called up to the lookout. He must have gotten a reply because he raised both hands, thumbs up, and turned away, shouting orders.

Marty saw the gun ports open and the six-pounders run out. *I bloody hope he kept the gunners on board*, he thought.

They came up to the point, and Marty put an extra man on each sweep. That gave them about an extra quarter knot.

"We must be doing all of two knots now," he said to Tom, "let's hope they be rotten shots because we be fish in a barrel."

"Well, we be about to find out," said Tom, nodding to the guns.

The middle Howitzer fired first, and they heard the shot whistle overhead and there was a bang as it exploded about forty yards past them.

"Exploding shells?" Marty yelled at Tom, "this is bloody dangerous!"

Tom laughed and said, "Trust the bloody army to come up with something like that."

The second gun fired, and this one exploded close enough that some of the shrapnel landed on their deck. No one was hit but it scared the hell out of them. The third gun fired, and Marty yelled, "EVERYONE GET DOWN!"

This time, it was right over their heads and there was a hail of shrapnel as it burst over the fore deck. Two men were left screaming in agony from hits and the foremast had a number of bites taken out of it.

Then there was the thunder of a broadside being loosed as the Snipe opened with her six-pounders. Marty got to his feet and looked towards the headland. All but one of the shots went wide and that one hit short, directly in line with the guns, ricocheting up and taking out two men.

There was a cordon of infantry along the shore about thirty feet away, and they let fly with a musket volley that, thankfully, went mostly high.

"To the Larboard side!" he yelled, "Get a pistol!"

He knew the chances of hitting anything at that range was remote, but his marines were already there and taking aim with their muskets.

"Hold Fire!" he ordered and waited until the men were all ready.

"Take aim! FIRE!"

The cloud of smoke was impressive as most of the men had two pistols each and there were the 6 muskets as well. He heard at least one scream from the shore, so somebody had scored a hit.

That got them enough time to get around the point. The French howitzers traversed and fired again, but they had spoiled the range and the shots went over. The Snipe opened again, but Marty couldn't see what the result was as they had made the turn around the headland and were entering the estuary proper.

As they cleared the lee of the land, they found a Southerly breeze, and Marty called for sails to be set and the sweeps to be run in. The men who had manned them were exhausted and collapsed to the deck. Marty looked for Bill and saw him propped by the mainmast with his left arm in a sling. He saw Marty looking and raised his right and waved. Marty grinned back and then concentrated on steering them out of there.

They made it to sea without further incident, and Marty handed over the wheel to John Smith, and walked over to Bill.

"You OK?" he asked as he dropped to the deck beside him.

"Been better," Bill replied. "Are all your adventures so bloody dangerous?" he asked with a grin.

"Yup, so far they have and this one wasn't anywhere near the worst," Marty answered, "but it is fun though, isn't it," he added with a laugh.

Bill started to laugh, "Fun! You call this bloody fun!" he laughed harder, and Marty joined him until they were leaning against each other laughing till they hiccupped and then one or the other would say "Fun!" and they would start again. Soon the laughter had spread right around the ship.

On the Snipe, Armand caught the sound as it carried back on the wind. He shook his head and smiled to himself.

Chapter 9: Horse Trading

Once back in harbour and securely tied up, they said goodbye to the smugglers and started taking inventory of what they had stolen. They still had the harbour watch that the French had left on board and a young woman, the one Marty had heard scream. The men would be handed over to the Navy proper and dealt with appropriately. The young woman was offered the chance to continue her business in Deal under the supervision of a local madam, she would be a novelty and make good money.

The guns that had been left on the Alouette were useless. The barrels honeycombed and more dangerous to the gun crew than the target. So, they just piled them on the shore and left them. The fore mast was chipped by shrapnel but was sound enough and could continue to be used and the rigging was easily repaired. All in all, they had a serviceable ship.

They decided not to report her capture to the admiralty as they figured the Navy would take her away from them if they did and that would defeat the whole purpose of the exercise.

A couple of days later, Marty took a horse and rode to Chatham to see a man who was purported to be a dealer in everything and was recommended to him by one of the smugglers. As Marty rode up to the address he had been given, he found himself approaching a well-appointed medium size house in a 'nice' area with a well-kept flower garden in front of it.

He got off his horse, looped his reins through a hitching ring and went to the front door. He was about to knock when the door opened and a man in an old red smoking jacket and a blue and black tapestry smoking cap stood looking at him.

"Mr. Fletcher?" Marty asked.

"Who wants to know?" the man replied.

"A friend of the free traders," Marty responded as he had been instructed.

The man looked around, checking that Marty was alone, then beckoned him inside. The house was clean, tidy, and tastefully furnished. There were no servants that he could see as he followed the man into a library.

Fletcher sat at a desk and indicated Marty should sit in an armchair near to it. Marty noted that he was now lower than Fletcher and had to look up to him.

I will have to remember this trick, he thought.

"Well, what can I do for you Mr….?" he asked.

"Stockley, Martin Stockley," Marty replied, "I am told you can get anything for the right price."

"Most things, most things," Fletcher smiled in reply and sat back with his hands clasped across his stomach.

"Well, I am in need of some ships cannon," Marty said.

"Really? They can be awful hard to come by. What size and how many did you have in mind?" Fletcher asked, taking out a sheet of paper and picking up a pen.

Marty smiled, took a sheet of paper from his inside pocket, and handed it over.

"Let me see," said Fletcher as he read the list.

"Twelve twenty-four-pound carronades plus cannister, bar, and round shot."

"Eighteen, French, nine-pound cannon plus round, bar, chain shot, and cannister."

"Four thirty-six-pound carronades plus cannister, bar, and round shot."

"Sixty French sea-service-pattern muskets."

"Two thousand ball and cartridges for the muskets."

"Ten tons of Navy standard powder."

"Are you fighting a private war? No, don't answer that. I don't need to know. How will you pay? This is an expensive list."

"Half now in gold and the rest on delivery," Marty replied.

Fletcher looked at him appraisingly, "and how am I to trust its quality?"

Marty opened the saddle bag he had carried in over his shoulder and took out a pouch, which clinked. He tossed it onto the desk and said,

"Well, I reckon you could test it and weigh it if that would satisfy you."

Fletcher looked surprised but reached out and picked up the pouch, weighing it in his hand as he opened the draw string. He tipped the contents on the desk. Gold coins slid over each other.

"Hmm, French Louis d'Or," he selected one at random and bit it. Satisfied, he got out a pair of goldsmith's scales and weighed it. He then selected another and did the same.

"They seem to be the genuine article," he said, "your order will cost three thousand in total, including carriage. So, I will require one thousand five hundred pounds in advance." He sat back with a smug smile on his face.

"Oh, I don't think so," said Marty, "The French guns would have been sold for scrap, and the carronades diverted from Navy yards at ten bob on the pound at most. I reckon we are looking at a fair price of fifteen hundred pound, which will give you a fair profit," he pulled out two more pouches of coins and then one more.

"That's the equivalent of seven hundred and fifty pound there on the table."

"Don't get smart with me you whippersnapper," snarled Fletcher, "two thousand five hundred be the price."

Marty sat back, letting his coat fall open, letting the grips of his pistols poke out. He made no move to touch them and made no threat. He just waited.

The silence stretched out. Marty didn't move, he just looked at Fletcher, who was looking more uncomfortable by the minute.

Then Marty reached forward and took two gold pieces off the table and dropped them in his saddle bag. Fletcher looked surprised and another minute ticked by. Marty reached forward and went to take another two coins when Fletcher put his hands over the pile and hissed.

"Ok! Fifteen hundred, you devil's spawn," and pulled the pile of money towards him.

They filled in the details of the deal. The goods would be delivered in two weeks by barge as shifting it by road would be too conspicuous.

Marty stood as the deal was concluded and held out his hand for Fletcher to shake. The old man looked him in the eye, took it, and said,

"Where in God's creation did a youngster like you learn to negotiate like that?"

"Why, I be from Dorset and we be all 'orse traders from down thar, ya know," he replied in full dialect with a wink.

Fletcher laughed, put his hand on his shoulder, and said,

"When you have finished doing what you be doing with the brotherhood, come see me. I could use a man like you, we could make a lot of money together."

Marty took his time on the return trip. He still had gold in his saddlebags, but he was heavily armed with two saddle pistols as well as his Nocks, so he wasn't overly concerned with highwaymen. He stopped at an Inn for the night and was eating his meal when an older scruffily dressed midshipman walked in with a trio of burly bosun's mates.

The press had come calling. There was no point in running as he knew they would have all the exits covered.

The mid looked around the room, and his eyes settled on Marty, who was dressed in nondescript travel cloths that were intended to make him blend in.

Marty knew what was coming next, so he leaned back in his chair and waited.

"Him will do fur starters."

"I wouldn't do that," Marty said in his best Navy voice.

"Fuck you," the mid said and waved his men forward.

They stopped dead when a pistol appeared in Marty's hand and pointed directly between the mid's eyes.

"I said you don't want to do that if you want yer man here to keep the top of his head," said Marty, and reached into his inside coat pocket to produce a paper. He waved it at the mid.

"You can read, can't you?" he said in his most insulting tone. The mid nodded and started to reach out.

"Don't even think it," he said to the left-hand mate who leaned forward as if he would make a lunge.

"Stay still, you idiot," barked the mid who had developed a sheen of sweat on his forehead. He reached forward carefully, took the paper, and opened it without noting the seal. He read it, blinked, and read it again.

"Stand down," he growled to his men. "He be under admiralty protection."

The men backed up a step and relaxed.

"Better," Marty said and held out his hand for the paper.

When he got it back, he un-cocked his pistol and put it away.

"You had better try another pub. This one is under protection tonight," he said with a smile.

The mid glared at him but jerked his head towards the door and said, "come on lads."

The landlord came over to him and practically bowed at his feet.

"Thankee sir," he said, "them devils have been raiding us every week for two month now. People are getting afraid to come 'ere."

"Well, it's safe for tonight," Marty said, "they won't bother you again."

"Can I get you summit, sir? I have a lovely brandy, just in if you knows what I mean."

Marty nearly laughed out loud.

The next morning, he rose early and went to the window to check on the weather. He noticed someone in what looked like a Navy pea coat leaning against a wall in a spot that overlooked the stables. Curious, he carefully checked the surroundings he could see from the window, without exposing himself. He caught a glimpse of a second figure a short way away, standing tucked into the mouth of an alley.

"I bet there's two more around the back somewhere as well," he said to himself.

He got dressed and made sure all his weapons were primed and ready. He also dug into the bottom of his saddlebags and retrieved a gift he had from Bill Clarence after the cutting out of the Corvette. A blackjack, a leather-bound bag of lead shot with a handle, and a loop of leather to secure it to the wrist. It was a vicious weapon used to silence people with a sharp blow to the head, but it could also be used in a general melee to great effect.

He went downstairs and dropped his saddlebags behind the bar in the common room. The inn keeper appeared, and Marty put his finger to his lips in a shush. He whispered in his ear, told him about the men outside and added,

"they be the press from last night. I reckon they be waiting for to teach me a lesson."

He then whispered a few instructions and went back through the inn's kitchen to the back door. He cracked it very slowly inwards and peeked through the gap. No one to the left but the stables were to the right, so he opened it further hoping it didn't creak or squeak until he could get his head through enough to peek to the right. There was one of the Bosun's mates armed with a club and a rattan cane.

So, it's a beating I'm in for, he thought.

Well, he would see about that. He opened the door enough so he could slip out and crept up behind the man. He put his toe down first on every step and carefully lowered his heel to make no noise. Just like stalking rabbits when he was younger. He came up behind the man and with a flick of his wrist, hit him behind the right ear with the blackjack. He dropped like a stone. Marty caught him before he hit the ground and pulled him back to the door. He took off the sailor's coat, and, using some lengths of cord he had looped through his belt, tied the unconscious man's arms behind his back and his ankles together.

He pulled on the coat and picked up the hat that was lying where it had fallen and put it on. He edged up to the corner and looked around it, he could see another man stood at the corner of the stable where he wouldn't be seen by someone approaching from the front door of the inn.

Marty pulled up the collar and pulled down the brim of the hat and just walked across to him.

"What be you doin', Jack?" said the second man and as Marty got up to him, he said in surprise, "You ain't, Jack!" and raised his club.

Marty flicked out with the blackjack, catching him on the knuckles, and the club dropped out of fingers that were probably broken. Before he could scream, Marty kneed him in the groin and then rapped him on the back of the head. Thirty seconds later, he had him tied up and had shoved his own grubby rag of a handkerchief in his mouth as a gag.

A quick glance up past the stables showed that no one had heard anything. He grinned, went back to the kitchen door, and gave a low whistle.

He went back to the place where the first man had been and waited. He heard the front door of the Inn slam, and a figure came around the corner wearing his overcoat and a hat with a wide brim that he would never wear. It was, in fact, the innkeeper who had volunteered to spring the trap. As he approached the stable door, Marty saw two figures come through the gate and follow at a discreet distance.

The innkeeper entered the stables, and the two men sped up to close in. As they got up to it, the old mid beckoned for the two men he thought were waiting further down to approach.

Marty stepped out and as soon as he was seen by the two at the door, they stepped inside. He ran over to the door as soon as they entered and followed them in.

He saw the innkeeper throwing the saddlebags at the two men as they went at him with clubs raised. Marty stepped up behind the mate and cracked him behind the ear, dropping him like a rock. He then pulled his pistol and turned to the mid, who turned to face him in astonishment and then fear as he saw the gun.

"Put down the club," Marty ordered.

The mid looked around, realized he was alone, and dropped it to the floor.

"Now, I want your name and ship," demanded Marty.

"Midshipman Gareth Moore, off the Invincible," he replied.

"How old are you?" Marty asked.

"Thirty-two."

Only good for the press, Marty thought, at thirty-two years old he would never be made lieutenant.

"You want to spend the rest of your life on the beach?" he asked.

Moore shook his head. Being beached would leave him with nothing as midshipmen didn't get paid if they weren't on ship.

"If you had looked at the seal on that protection, you would have seen it came from the First Naval Lord who I answer to directly. So, one word from me and you will be washed up ashore with no pay for the rest of your miserable life. Understand?"

Moore nodded miserably.

"I'll make you a once in a lifetime offer. I will let you go and take your idiot mates with you if you give your word never to visit this pub again, never mention that this happened to anyone or that you saw me or the protection." Moore nodded vigorously.

"Be warned. If you or your mates tell anyone about this, you will all make friends with the Bridport Dagger for treason. Am I clear?"

Moore nodded again.

"Now, collect your rabble and get out of here," Marty ordered.

The innkeeper helped by pouring a bucket of water, that was for the horses to drink from, over the unconscious man's head. It was ice cold, and he woke, spluttering. Moore grabbed him and dragged him to his feet and out of the stable.

The innkeeper started to laugh. "Well that's one press gang we don't have to worry about anymore," he chuckled. "What's a Bridport dagger?" he asked, taking off Marty's coat and handing it over.

"A hangman's noose made of best Bridport rope," Marty replied as he stripped off the Mate's coat and pulled on his own.

He made his goodbyes and led his horse out into the yard just as the four men left heading back up the road towards Chatham. He mounted and headed South.

Once back at the farm, he reported to Armand and caught up on what had been going on. They had received another "package" to deliver to France that had been delivered to Brest the night before. Armand had accompanied it.

They had also had a visit from William Wickham. He was satisfied with the arrangement with the smugglers and said,

"Admiral Hood was concerned that you didn't inform him about the acquisition of the Corvette in advance, but would 'legitimize' it by buying it in."

"How the hell did Hood find out about the Corvette so fast?" Marty gasped when they were alone.

"One of the men he sent us must be informing him," Arnaud concluded, "it would be just like him to want to keep the eye on us."

"Does this change our plans?" Marty asked.

"Non, mon amie, Monsieur Wickham says we are part of 'is dirty tricks world now and 'e likes the plan, but when we sell off the goods, to let the smugglers do it so it cannot be traced back to the government. Oh, and to make sure the Admiral gets his cut!"

Armand was surprised that Marty had gotten the weapons for fifteen hundred and laughed when Marty told him about taking the two gold pieces back for every minute he didn't agree.

"I want you to oversee the modifications to the Snipe to receive the carronades. We need the help of a carpenter, non?" he said once he stopped laughing.

"Aye, I reckon we do. I saw a boatyard further up the river. I think I'll go for a visit and see what they be like," replied Marty.

The next morning saw him walking up the riverbank to a boatyard with a number of half-built fishing boats and a couple of complete ones ready for launch.

He wandered in and called out, "Ahoy the boatyard, anybody aboard?"

A man in a working smock with shoulders that would have done Hercules proud stepped in to view and said,

"Aye, and what can I do fer you?"

Marty figured that a more rural accent than his Navy voice would work better here, so he dropped into his Dorset accent.

"How be 'e master shipwright. I be lookin' fer a man 'o can 'elp me with makin' some new guns fit me Cutter like," he said.

"That would be the cutter moored down at the 'arbor then would it?" he said with a smile, "You be the boys who have teamed wi' Bill down at Deal aint ya?"

"Aye, that be us," Marty admitted, "I be Martin," he added and held out his hand.

"I'm Mike. I 'eard of you. You be the one wi' the big knife," he said, shaking his hand with a grip of iron.

"Word do get around," Marty laughed.

"Now, be you the man to 'elp us?"

"You pay in hard coin?" he asked.

"Aye, I will give a quarter up front fer good will and the rest when the job's done. We will have plenty o' werk fer 'e over time if we can get along like."

"A third up front and when do we start?" he replied, shaking Marty's hand once he agreed in his crushing grip.

Damn, if he keeps that up, I'm going to need a doctor, thought Marty.

After an inspection and a detailed description of what needed to be changed to replace the six pounders with carronades, they haggled over a price and finally came to an agreement. Marty handed over a third straight away and for the next week, the sound of sawing and hammering echoed around the harbour as the carpenter, aided by the more carpentry able hands, worked on the Snipe.

A Thames barge was spotted running into the estuary on Friday morning. The huge red sail looked like the sun coming up from the East as it slowly got closer and stood at the bow was a man in a shabby red smoking jacket and hat. Marty grinned and said to Armand,

"Our guns have just arrived."

Every man was pulled in to unload the cargo. Sheerlegs were set up on the dock and used to lift the heavy barrels and carriages off the barge. Once they were ashore, they were inspected by Marty and Armand and moved up the dock to be next to their designated ships. The muskets and ammunition were loaded into a cart and taken to the secure armoury at the farm and the powder to a magazine that was isolated from the farm and dock in a large cellar like hole they had dug, lined and roofed with wood, a layer of canvas and finally sod. The shot was stored in a shed by the dock.

Once the barge had been completely unloaded and the delivery inspected and tallied off, Marty, Armand, and Fletcher went to the farm for something to eat and to settle the bill. Over a plate of fresh crusty bread and a selection of ham, cheese, and pickles, they talked and got to know each other. Fletcher had no problem that Armand was French. He didn't ask any questions about their background and accepted their story that they were setting up as privateers with Bill and his boys.

They settled up the balance of the money they owed him and talked about the war and domestic politics. Finally, he asked, "How are you planning on disposing of the goods that you obtain from privateering?"

"Bill will take care of that, but I can tell him you have an interest if you want," answered Marty.

"I would appreciate that, my boy," Fletcher smiled, "and don't forget what I said. When you finish playing pirates come see me."

It took another week to mount all the guns and, carefully, load the two ships with powder and ammunition.

The Marines were not happy with the French muskets, but Marty explained that they were going to pretend to be a French ship and it would look a little odd if they were carrying the distinctive navy pattern Brown Bess. The problem of French pistols was solved by Bill who told them they had picked up a load of them in France. They didn't ask why or how.

The next step was to get a crew together from Deal and train them in sailing a sloop or, as they kept reminding themselves, a corvette. They didn't want them to sail Navy style as no privateer, especially a French one, would sail like that. However, they still had to learn the rigging, the sail drills and how to handle the guns. That took a couple of months and Marty and Armand took it in turns commanding as only one of them could be away at any time. The other having to tend to the sending and receiving of packages.

Finally, by late November they felt confident to go to sea and put into practice what had been learned. When they finally left, with Marty in command, the weather was variable to say the least. In the Channel, it wasn't too bad as the weather was coming from the Northwest, but as they got down towards Cherbourg, it started to get really rough with gale force winds and huge seas.

After a brief consultation with the master's mate, Marty decided to head for the Channel Islands and try for a landing at Saint Peter Port on Guernsey. The men fought the weather gallantly and when they got close, they had the choice to go between Guernsey and Herm Island, a gap that was less than two and a half miles wide or go around Herm which would put them directly into the wind to get into port.

One of the Deal boys, Ken Boyce, spoke up and said he had made the run in to St Peter Port many times and offered to pilot them in. He recommended that they run the gap between the islands even though it was getting dark.

They got closer and reduced sail to double reefed topsails, but it still felt like they were flying. As they passed through the gap, they could see Guernsey on the starboard side with Herm on their port and as they moved into the lee of the island the wind dropped noticeably and the waves reduced a little.

They needed to make the turn from South by Southwest to Southwest just at the right moment to enter the harbour and it was one of the tensest moments of Marty's short career. But Boyce made the entry as if he did it every day and as they passed the wall, he put them into the wind and dropped the anchor. It was then that Marty looked up to see the Tricolour of France still flying from the stern. He quickly pulled it down and ordered the British flag raised instead.

As they sat at anchor waiting for the storm to pass, Marty reviewed the performance of the men with his master's mate. All in all, they concluded that they had pulled together during the storm and were forming into a coherent crew. They needed more practice with the guns, but the storm had done them a favour by melding the crew into one.

The next morning, a boat pulled out from the shore and came directly to them. A tall slim man came up the side, boarded, and asked to speak to the captain. He came down into the cabin and looked around. He saw Marty and dismissing him as a cabin boy, said to the sailor who brought him down,

"Well, where is he?"

"Where is who?" said Marty.

"The captain," the man said.

"Here," said Marty.

"Where?" said the man.

"Here," said Marty, pointing at his chest.

"You?" He said incredulously.

"Yup me," said Marty.

"But you be but a boy," said the man.

Marty looked at him steadily for a moment, took a deep breath to control his temper, and said,

"Shall we start again? My name is Martin Stockley, Captain and part owner of the Alouette. And who do I have the pleasure of addressing?" he held his hand out.

"Stuart English, Harbour Master," he replied with a disbelieving expression on his face but shook the offered hand.

"You came into harbour in somewhat of a hurry last night, and we noticed you had a French flag flying for a while there and this is a French built ship, so you can understand that we are somewhat curious."

Marty went to the desk and took a document from the drawer. He took it to English and offered it to him.

"That should explain things," he said.

English opened the paper and read it.

"A Letter of Marque," he said, "so you are privateers."

"That's us," Marty said, "we had a notion to poach in the Frenchie's back yard."

"Well, you're in the right area then. There be a fair bit of traffic between Brest and pretty much everywhere that's avoiding the blockade."

"Good! Glad to hear that. Have you seen any come through here?" Marty asked.

"No French, only some neutrals, a couple of Americans, and a Dane in the last week. They don't do any business here as they can make much more from the French," he replied with more than a hint of dissatisfaction.

"What goods do they have that you want?" Marty asked on a hunch.

"Tobacco, cotton, hemp, sugar," he said, "we can use them all and export what we don't."

"So, if we come across any then . . ." said Marty and raised an eyebrow.

"We wouldn't ask where they came from," was the reply with a grin.

"Is it too early for a Brandy?" asked Marty, "to 'seal the deal. I have a very nice Armagnac from Normandy."

"Not at all," Stuart replied.

An hour later, Stuart English left the Alouette swaying slightly and humming happily to himself. Marty waved to him from the side then very deliberately turned and walked, almost directly, back to his cabin.

Several coffees later, he came back on deck with more than a slight headache. In fact, the light hurt his eyes. The weather had cleared a lot and he figured it was time to get back to sea. The tide was slack, and the wind was from the Southwest, which was perfect for leaving harbour but not for heading down to Brest as he had planned.

They left directly and headed Northwest towards Plymouth to get enough Westing to tack South to Roscoff. They practiced with the guns and in Marty's opinion, were slightly faster than the equivalent French crew but way slower than a full Navy crew. But that was alright he didn't want to get in a shooting match with anybody unless he could get close enough to use his smashers.

They reached Plymouth the following morning and turned South, as close to the wind as they could. It was glorious sailing weather and with du Demaine on board the food was way better than standard Navy fare. They were in sight of the French coast when they turned Northwest again

They were about mid channel when the cry went up from the masthead, "Sail Ho! Fine on the larboard beam. Looks like a Schooner."

Marty grabbed a glass and ran up the mainmast ratlines. He went around the futtock shrouds and settled on the spar next to the lookout. He scanned the horizon first and then looked for the speck of sail. There it was! Travelling Southeast and looked to be heading towards Brest.

"Wear ship!" called Marty down to the deck, "course two points West of South."

He descended to the deck via a stay, and called his mates to him, "remember, if she be a Yankee trader, we will stop him as if we are a French privateer. Everyone who doesn't speak French is to stay silent, and I only want to see French made guns on show. Get the carronades loaded but keep them covered. Tom, get the Basque boys, Wilson and du Demaine together along with any others who can speak French. You will be the boarding party."

He then went to the sergeant of marines, made sure they had swapped their Brown Bess's for French muskets, and reminded them not to form up in ranks

The two ships were on a converging course and now the Schooner was hull up they could see she was Yankee built.

Marty had the ship cleared for action and the starboard battery manned and loaded but not run out. The men stayed down out of sight. America was officially neutral, but everyone knew that the Republican faction was sympathetic to the revolution and were supplying the French with everything they could in spite of the 'official' prohibition of their Federalist government.

As they closed, they could see the crew of the other ship watching them and one even waved. When they were two cables apart, Marty ordered the guns run out and a shot to be put under her bow. That caused a flurry of activity on the schooner, which dropped her main sail and hove to. They came up within half a cable and kept her under their guns.

Marty let Antton lead the boarding party and stayed on board to keep a French speaker available. A few minutes after the boys had boarded, he saw the schooner's crew herded to the foredeck. He could see one man waving his arms and complaining loudly. He could just about hear him from the Alouette. He was gesticulating to the Alouette and looked to be asking to be taken across. He was out of luck. Marty had given clear instructions that the boarding party should pretend that they didn't speak English.

Antton came to the rail and shouted across to Marty in French, *"They are American and are carrying coffee, sugar, molasses, and Tobacco. The boat is old but well maintained."*

Marty called back, *"They can keep the boat. I will pull alongside and transfer the cargo."*

He then shouted orders in French; he had drilled the crew in a few key phrases, and they manoeuvred so the two ships could be tied alongside each other.

The American crew were shut in the cable locker out of the way then the ship was systematically looted of the cargo and anything else of value. Marty felt a little odd about taking the personal valuables of the crew, but it was what a privateer would do.

When they were finished, they loosened some vital parts of the rigging to buy them time to get away and unlocked the door to the cable tier. They left the ship quietly and sailed off with the wind on their quarter heading Northeast. Marty looked back, and could see the crew of the schooner had come up on deck. The skipper climbed the ratlines shaking his fist at their disappearing stern shouting profanities and threats in equal measure.

They headed home rather than to Guernsey. Marty wanted to report back to Armand. He also had in mind that the Deal boys weren't used to being away for long cruises, and he needed to break them in gently.

As they got into English waters, they raised the British colours and the Alouette changed to the Swan. When they finally moored up, the Snipe was missing, and Marty went to The Farm to see what was up. Their Steward came to meet him at the door and told him the Lieutenant Armand had taken the Snipe out as one of the fishing boats was late back from picking up a package in Calais. They didn't think there was much chance of finding it, but they knew its route and hoped for the best.

He grabbed a quick coffee and headed back to the dock. Unloading was going well, and John Smith was tallying up the cargo as it was unloaded. He saw Bill Clarence stood talking to a couple of his men. His arm was out of the sling from his and he looked fit.

"Hello Bill, come to check we ain't cheating you," said Marty with a laugh.

"Well, it wouldn't do to give you too long a rein, would it?" he joked back. "Not a bad haul. That little lot should make us a few bob."

"Easy money," said Marty.

Tom walked over, "Them yanks were bloody furious," he grinned, "Their Cap'ain kept asking to see ours, but we just kept on with 'we don't speeek Englaise'. Which pissed him off even more. He even said that he and the French were allies."

"Makes them fair game then," said Marty, "We got copies of their papers and took their bill of lading. Seems that they are part of a consortium, whatever one of them be."

"Means that they belong to a group of like-minded individuals," said a familiar voice from behind him

Marty nearly jumped out if his skin!

"Mr. Wickham, please don't do that," he gasped.

Wickham laughed, "you should always keep one eye over your shoulder in this game," he said.

Marty asked, "Why are you here?"

"Just checking on my favourite prodigy," he replied.

Marty wasn't sure what that meant or even if it referred to him or Armand.

"You have been busy, I see," Wickham observed.

Marty reached into his coat pocket and took out a sheaf of papers. "These are for you. I was going to get them sent up to London tomorrow."

"Thank you," said Wickham.

"Now, I need to talk to you alone for a while."

Marty looked at Bill and said, "Can I leave you to get this lot stowed away?"

Bill nodded and waved for him to go.

Chapter 10: A Little Bird

Back at the farm, they went into the bureau, as Armand called the small room where they ran things from. Marty invited Wickham to sit in one of the comfortable armchairs.

"I have a mission for you. It is one of high importance and needs to be done as soon as possible. You must not wait for Armand to return as we don't have time for that."

Marty was intrigued and leaned forward to hear more.

"We have gained access to a list of French agents in England and it was being carried from Paris by one of our people when she was arrested in Amiens en route to Calais. Luckily, she carried the list in her head, or she would be dead by now. She is being held by the secret police in their headquarters in the town. We don't know if she was arrested because they knew she was a spy or just because they suspect she comes from an aristo family." Wickham explained.

"And you want me to go and get her out," Marty said.

"Yes," said Wickham, "I would advise you take a small team with all the skills you will need for a jailbreak. Just one or two men if you can manage it."

Marty thought about the problem for a minute or two.

"What do we know about the secret police building?"

"It is in the centre of town next to the Hotel de Ville, the Townhall. It is guarded around the clock by secret police personnel and prisoners are kept in the cellar, which is a combined dungeon and torture chamber."

"Piece of cake then," said Marty sarcastically.

Wickham ignored that.

"Here is a map of the town centre, and I have marked the police headquarters on it. Here is a plan of the ground floor, well as much as our people could see from the entry."

Marty took the map and plan, studying them for a good ten minutes.

"This building here," he said, pointing to a building to the West of the place de Hotel de Ville, "Is that a barracks?"

Wickham looked at the map, "Yes, for a regiment of cavalry."

"So, they will have stables and an armoury then," said Marty.

"I should think so," said Wickham.

"I think I have a plan," murmured Marty.

Twelve hours later, Marty, Matai, Wilson, and Roland were in a fishing boat manned by the smugglers, heading to a landing at Le Crotoy on the estuary of the river Somme. It would have been easier to land at St. Valery, but they thought their faces may be recognised there after the theft of the Alouette.

Roland had figured he needed a good lockpick (himself), a good knife man (Matai), someone who was good with explosives (Roland), and some muscle (Wilson) who could also speak French.

They would travel inland from Le Crotoy, which was the nearest landing to Amiens, rescue the agent, then exit back to Le Crotoy to be picked up by the Deal boys and home. What could possibly go wrong?

The landing was regulation, and they were met by a 'friend" who supplied them with identification and travel papers. Then after a quick meal, they were on their own. Marty knew that all they had to do was follow the river and they would find Amiens. The only problem was the river passed through numerous villages and the town of Abbeville, which meant they would have to negotiate a number of checkpoints. They needed a cover story and the best they had come up with was that they were stone masons who were travelling to Paris via Amiens. They managed to get a couple of tool bags with hammers and stone chisels, which were a convenient place to hide their weapons, to complete their disguise. The smugglers provided them with fake papers.

It worked quite well as they passed through the numerous checkpoints without too much trouble. Three men and a boy didn't attract much attention, and Roland played the part of gang boss to a tee. As they approached the entry to Amiens, they got a more severe grilling, but the well-rehearsed, simple cover story stood up to examination and they got through. Once inside the town, they headed to a guest house that they had been assured was run by a sympathiser to the royalist cause.

The house was on the Rue Saint-Martin aux Wades not too far from the centre of town and they found it by asking directions of a couple of surly townsfolk. The overriding impression was of a town under siege. The difference though was that instead of the siege coming from the outside, here it was inflicted on the town from within. There was an all-pervading feeling of fear and of everyone watching everyone else. It was very uncomfortable.

Marty went to the Place de L'Hotel de Ville and the first things he saw were the Tree of Liberty and the Guillotine. His timing couldn't have been worse as he arrived just as an execution was about to take place and there was a large crowd. A cart drawn by a worn-out nag came into the square with a man dressed as a baker in the back. He had a wild look and was protesting his innocence in a loud voice.

Marty asked a man who stood nearby what crime he had committed to warrant such a punishment. The man laughed and told him that his 'crime' was to be too successful. He had been denounced as a traitor by one of his competitors.

It seems in France to get ahead, you risk losing your head, thought Marty.

His attention was drawn back to the drama in front of them. The man was dragged on to the platform and forced to stand against a plank which came up to his shoulders. Straps were tightened around his thighs and chest then the plank was pivoted to the horizontal, eliciting a terrified squawk from the condemned man.

Ingenious, thought Marty.

It was slid forward until the man's neck was directly under the blade. A proclamation was read stating that the man had been found guilty of treason to the state and the rope holding the blade at the top of its slide was released.

THUNK, and it was all over. The crowd cheered without a huge amount of enthusiasm as the executioner held up the head by the hair, then everyone started home.

The square was surrounded on three sides by a building in a U with the open end to the South. The secret police were based at the end of the Western arm of the U. The entrance was at the South end and a pair of, what looked like, doormen were stationed outside, but Marty wasn't fooled, they were armed policemen. He walked casually past. The building had the Rue de la Malmaison running up the West side. The Rue Gresset ran past the main entrance at the South end. As far as he could see, that was the only outside entrance to the police part of the building. The East side looked over the square. There were windows, but all the ones on the ground floor had bars. He decided to return to the guest house.

Once there, he met up with the other guys who had been looking around the surrounding area. Their reports were more encouraging. There was a barracks, and it was for cavalry. They had identified the armoury, which was a room at the end of the stables that had just one guard. This was good as the French cavalry carried carbines so there would be ammunition in there.

He described the police building to his men, and they started to work over the problem. They rapidly concluded that walking into the front door wasn't practical. So, how could they get in – and out again?

Wilson asked, "You say it is all one building around the square. Maybe there is a connecting door from the police part to the town hall or at least there was one at some time."

"That's a good point," said Marty, "Roland, go ask our host how the building was used before the revolution."

Roland left the room, and the rest continued looking at maps and discussed the merits of different escape routes. Roland came back with a smile on his face.

"Before the revolution, the entire building was owned by the local Count and was 'is town 'ouse. After the revolt, they commandeered it for L'Hotel de Ville and when the committee in Paris installed the secret police here, they took over the Southwest wing as their headquarters."

"So, there will be doors or there were doors that connected the two," said Marty.

"Yes," Said Roland, "but there is more. The count was a bon vivant and had an extensive wine cellar. The story is that when he was beheaded the whole town stayed drunk on it for days. An exaggeration but it means that . . ."

"The cellar went right under the whole house!" finished Marty and grinned at his team, "We have our way in."

The next day, Marty and Antton visited l'Hotel de Ville on the pretext of extending their stay as one of their men was ill. They took note of the entrance and the windows, the security, the location of the staircases, and what doors led off in which direction. They wandered down towards the West wing on the pretext that they were looking for a particular office and found a door without a label on it. They opened it and found it was a cupboard.

A man who had been watching them from an office door approached them and asked.

"what are you doing?"

Roland told him they were there to check the floor supports in the cellar as some cracks had been reported, and they were looking for the way down to check that the floor was properly supported. The man looked alarmed and told them to take the next corridor to the right then the second door on the left and they would be right there.

They thanked him and got his name, Monsieur Blanc, and flattered him he must be someone important. To which he told them he was actually only a clerk in the works department.

They found the door and went down into the cellars. Cluttered didn't even begin to describe them as it looked as if every piece of defunct furniture had been dumped down there since the revolution.

They scrambled their way to the end, shifting furniture to make a path and found a fairly new wall.

"This is right at the base of the West wing" observed Matai in a whisper, *"and look the mortar is really soft. They didn't use enough lime."*

Marty took a knife and scraped a little away and whispered back, *"They are lucky that it doesn't fall down on its own, this mortar is really bad. But that will make it easy for us."*

They made their way out of the cellar, brushed each other down as they had collected a fair amount of dust and cobwebs, and found their way back to the entryway. It was amazing! Nobody took any notice of workmen. They all seemed to assume they were supposed to be there.

Back at the guest house, they finalized their plans. Marty, Wilson, and Matai were to take on the rescue while Roland prepared the escape route and diversions. They would enter L'Hotel de Ville tomorrow afternoon and get into position so they could hit the police HQ in the middle of the night.

They slept in the next morning and made sure they had a good lunch as they didn't know when they would get to eat next. Around mid-afternoon when the clerks and staff of the L'Hotel de Ville would be just getting back from lunch and be at their least attentive, they walked in through the main entrance. They sauntered through the building to the cellar entrance, entered, and Marty locked the door behind them.

They settled down to wait. They heard the footsteps of the staff walking the corridors above them as they left for the evening, and they waited a bit more.

Marty had found an instrument that midwives used to listen to babies' heartbeats inside their mothers in a shop in the town. It was a wooden trumpet like device with a small bell at one end and a bigger bell at the other. You stuck the big bell against what you wanted to listen to and your ear against the smaller. He held it against the wall and could hear movement on the other side. They waited.

After he had heard nothing for around an hour, they started carefully removing the mortar around one of the bricks.

Lucky, we decided on stonemasons as a disguise, thought Marty as they had all the tools they needed.

They were soon able to slide the brick out. After that, they made a hole big enough for even Wilson to crawl through. They were lucky, they had made the hole in the centre of the wall and it came out into the central corridor of the cells.

They pulled neckerchiefs up over their noses to hide their faces and crawled through. They had a small shuttered lanthorn with a reflector that shone a beam of light forward, and they moved from cell to cell looking in on the inmates. Most were men, and some were in far better condition than others. Some were asleep others just lay in their cots staring at the ceiling, some were crying.

They soon found a cell with a young woman in it. She looked to be fast asleep. Marty quickly picked the lock and entered. He gently shook her shoulder and when her eyes opened, he put his hand over her mouth to stifle a scream if she made one.

"I am a friend," he whispered in French, *"Which bird sings the sweetest?"* he removed his hand so she could reply.

"The Linnet," she replied.

"We are here to get you out," he told her, *"come with us."*

He helped her to her feet and passed her to Wilson, who led her down the corridor. She was obviously weak and needed to lean on him for support.

As Marty went down the corridor, he unlocked each of the cells in turn and called the occupants to come with him. Those that could walk he led to the hole in the wall and sent them through. He crawled through after them.

He checked his watch it was two A.M., they were on time.

They took the time to replace the bricks, it wouldn't fool anybody for long, but it might buy them a little more time.

He led the group up the stairs to the door into the West wing. He had them wait and went on alone to check if there was anybody around. It was empty, so he called them out and took them to the main entrance.

The exit was the trickiest part as there was only one door and that opened into the square. To leave the square, they had to get past the secret police headquarters. He would have liked to have used the same trick they had in Calais and left by a back window, but they were all barred and to remove the bars would make far too much noise.

Timing was now vital. They waited behind the doors while Marty unlocked them, he waited, glancing frequently at his watch. Three A.M. came - and went. He looked at Matai, who shrugged. Then there was a loud explosion followed shortly after by the pop of musket rounds. Marty opened the door and glanced outside.

"*NOW,*" he said and pushed the door open and beckoned the group through. After the last was out, he closed and locked the door and hurried after them. They made their way up the East side of the square keeping close to the wall. The sky on the other side of the building was lit up by a fire that cast a dark shadow where they crept along. There was shouting, and he could see men leaving the police headquarters and running along the Rue Delambre towards the fire.

Marty was counting in his head and when he reached one hundred and twenty, there was another explosion to the East. Matai split off and walked over to the entrance of the police headquarters where one man remained looking at the fire. Matai seemed to make a gesture and the man folded down to the ground. He was quickly dragged onto the shadows.

Marty turned to the group and said, *"You are free. Get away as fast as you can. Find people you can trust and hide. Now, GO!"*

They ran, or staggered away, as best as they could, and he immediately put them out of his mind as he turned to Linnet. He could see she was barely holding on, so he asked Wilson to carry her. Matai re-joined them.

"Let's go," Marty said.

A third explosion sounded to the South as they made their way Northwest towards the river. They moved as fast as they could and stayed in the shadows, stopping frequently when they saw anybody. They reached the river and followed the bank to the West until they came upon a low quay. They found a boat marked with a neckerchief tied around its mooring rope that was big enough to carry all of them. They boarded and waited.

Less than ten minutes later, du Demaine appeared and jumped in after untying the rope.

"That was fun," he said with a laugh.

"Yes, a real thrill!" said Marty, *"Make way."*

They ran out the oars and moved the boat out into the middle of the stream and let it drift with the current which was quite gentle at around two knots. Dawn saw them well out of town, and they rowed the boat along at a fair speed.

Marty realized that he had to decide whether to continue on the river or go across country. However, Linnet was in poor shape, she had been beaten quite severely in the prison if the bruises on her arms and legs, that he could see, were anything to go by. That made up his mind, they would stay on the river as long as they could.

They got almost as far as Abbeville when they heard from a local that there was a barrage across the river, put there by the Police who were searching for people that had escaped from Amiens prison.

"*That was bloody quick,*" said Wilson, "they *must have killed a couple of horses to get that set up so soon.*"

They went to the South bank. That wasn't ideal as they had arranged to be picked up in Le Crotoy, which was on the North. But they would figure that out once past Abbeville.

The reason he had chosen Wilson became clear once they got on shore. He picked up Linnet as if she weighed nothing and cradled her in his massive arms. She smiled up at him and they could see tears in his eyes.

"*Come on then,*" he said in a gruff voice, "*let's get a move on.*"

They covered a few miles before dark and found a barn to sleep in. They had packed rations in the boat, so had the makings of a cold supper and there was fresh water in a well. But they had to be careful because they could see the farmer was in the house close by and they didn't want anyone sounding an alarm or running to the police.

False dawn saw them heading West with the emerging sun at their backs. Wilson, carrying Linnet, refused any help. Matai scouted ahead.

Then they heard the sound they dreaded. Dogs.

Matai came back to them and said, *"There are six flics ahead and they have a couple of tracking dogs with them."*

Marty thought and visualised the map in his mind. They needed to get to the crossing at Gouy, which was about five miles beyond Aberville, to get over to the North bank and then it was another ten miles to get to Le Crotoy. What they really needed, he thought, was a horse and cart or a carriage *but if wishes were horses, no one would ever have to walk,* he thought.

He got Matai to take him up to where the police were waiting and from the cover of a nearby copse, up-wind of them, he could see them starting to set up a picnic for their lunch. They scouted for a way around them towards the river and found that the ground dropped away and was marshy. Not ideal but it may cover their scent.

They returned to the others and guided them down to the lower ground, but it was soon apparent that they were going nowhere fast, the ground was so soft they were knee deep before they knew it. They were forced to head back up the hill towards the police and just as they got clear of the mud, the sound of baying hunting dogs could be heard getting closer.

They were running out of choices. If they stopped and fought, they would give away their position but then again if they ran, they probably wouldn't get far either. Then an idea came to Marty.

"Any of you guys good with dogs?"

"I had some before the revolution," said Matai, *"we used to hunt in the mountains with them."*

"Ok," said Marty, *"this is what we will do . . ."*

Two of the policemen were being dragged along by the dogs who were having a great time and very enthusiastically tracking the smell of the prison that still clung to Linette. The other four were following along as best as they could, but they weren't fit and were blowing with the exertion.

The dogs veered towards a copse of trees and led them through a gate in a high hedge. The dogs went through dragging their handlers behind them. Then the two fittest and last of all the two fattest who, as they passed through the gate, looked like they had run into a clothesline as their upper bodies stopped dead and their legs shot forward from under them. They landed heavily, and two masked figures descended on them delivering swift blows to the head.

The second pair were so intent on keeping up with the dog handlers and their rampant wards that they didn't see the two masked men catching them up. They didn't even feel the impact of the black jacks expertly applied behind their ears.

The dog handlers were hanging on for grim death as the dogs charged into the copse and started circling a tree. The policemen looked up and could see a girl with very nice legs sitting on a branch not far up.

"Hey men, we have one here in a tree," called one without taking his eyes off her.

When there was no reply, he laughed and said, *"Ha, those fat idiots are probably down to crawling after us by now."*

He turned as he heard a noise behind him and froze as he found himself looking at the chest of the biggest man he had ever seen. He saw the fist coming but remembered nothing after it hit him squarely between the eyes. His friend never saw the broken branch that hit him on the head.

Matai was dressed in one of the dog handler's uniforms and was feeding the dogs bits of salami he'd found in the pockets making them friends for life. The rest of them were getting dressed in the police uniforms that they had stripped from the now conscious but tied up policemen. Marty stepped over to one of them and asked

"Which town are you from?" The man refused to answer.

Marty drew his knife and set the point just under his eye.

"Which - town?"

"Cambron," he replied in absolute terror.

"*Thank you,*" Marty said with a smile that froze the blood and replaced the gag. Then said,

"*Right men let's move. We need to get to St. Valery as soon as possible.*" It was an obvious deception, but anything was worth a try.

Wilson had retrieved Linnet from the tree and carried her again. He was not in uniform as none of them would fit him. Instead, he played the role of prisoner. Matai had the dogs trotting along happily beside him, and Marty and Roland strolled along behind them.

They avoided entering the town of Cambron by circling it to the South and headed to Gouy. When they got there, they entered a tiny Hamlet of half a dozen houses. They found a farm and banged on the door. The farmer answered and looked terrified when he saw policemen outside. Roland stepped forward and asked,

"*Are you a friend of the revolution?*"

The farmer nodded, fearful of what was to come.

"*Do you have a cart?*"

The farmer nodded.

"*Do you have a horse?*"

He nodded again.

"*The revolution will buy them off you.*"

He looked surprised; so did Marty, who mouthed, "*Buy?*" Roland ignored him and continued.

"*We have heard you are a good son of the revolution; we will not punish you by commandeering your horse and cart without compensation.*"

He held up a half Louis, and the farmer nodded and took it.

"Please be so kind as to harness the horse for us while we eat," he concluded.

The farmer hurried off.

"Are you crazy?" hissed Marty once he was out of earshot.

"Buy the cart?"

Roland smiled and said,

"You never know, we might start a trend."

Marty rolled his eyes to the sky and said, *"Why me?"*

From then on, the trip was much easier. The horse plodded along at a fast walking pace and they soon got to the bridge over the river, crossed it, and turned onto the road to Le Crotoy. Any checkpoints just waved them through as they assumed, they were transporting prisoners. No one thought to ask for their papers, they were police after all. Marty figured the dogs helped as well. They looked as mean as hell even if they were as soft as butter.

They arrived in Crotoy and made their way to a safe house that the smugglers had told them to go to on their return. It was a relief to get out of the police uniforms as they weren't particularly clean and smelt of sweat and garlic, but they didn't throw them away as they might come in useful at a later date.

The Ariadne was due the next day at the first high tide so all they could do was wait. Marty checked his weapons, unloaded, cleaned, and re-loaded his pistols with fresh charges, and cleaned his knives and sharpened them. Then all he could do was sit and wait.

He got really fidgety and hungry, so he decided to go to the market and buy some fresh food. He grabbed Roland and they sauntered down to the market square. They spotted at least two secret police loitering around, and they figured there would be more, but they carried on as if they belonged making sure they didn't stand out in any way. Marty even asked one policeman what was going on as they just got back from fishing. His unique talent in mimicking dialects paying dividends. They got told there had been a gaol break from Amiens and they were on the lookout for escaped prisoners. Marty asked if they were dangerous and said if he spotted anybody strange, he would be sure to report it.

They knew they were safe from betrayal in Crotoy as it was run by the smugglers, and they were known to be friends who were under protection. Nobody would cross the smugglers as their justice was swift and almost always terminal.

After a tasty and sustaining fish stew cooked by Roland with the help of a recovering Linnet, they settled down to sleep, only to be woken by a quiet knock on the door. Marty cracked it open to see Gaston, one of the smugglers. He let him in.

"Martin, we must move you immediately. The secret police are conducting a house-to-house search and will get to this house in less than an hour."

Marty quickly woke the rest and they were ready to leave in minutes.

"Where will you take us?" Marty asked.

"Somewhere they will never look," he answered with a wink.

They crept down the street and entered the graveyard. Gaston led them confidently to a large mausoleum which he circled until they came to a stone door. He felt along one edge and pushed. To everyone's surprise, there was a metallic click and the door silently swung open. Marty would have loved to examine the entrance mechanism in detail, but it was too dark and anyway Gaston hurried them all inside and shut the door behind them. The darkness was profound. In fact, Marty had never experienced such total darkness before. There was the scrape of a flint and a flare as some tinder caught and then a lantern glowed to life. Marty could see that they were in a square room with several tombs in a row down one side.

"The mausoleum of the local lord and magistrate," Gaston said as he handed the lantern to Wilson and searched the floor. After a few seconds, he bent down and inserted a metal bar with a right-angled piece about one inch long at one end and a T-bar at the other into a hole, turned it ninety degrees, and pulled.

A trapdoor opened, revealing a flight of stairs. Gaston took back the lantern and led them down. The air got cooler and damper as they descended, they heard a thump behind them that they guessed was the trapdoor closing on its own. The bottom of the stairs opened up into a large cavern stacked with everything from wine and brandy to bales of silk and tobacco.

"Welcome to our storehouse," Gaston said with a bow. *"Come, we have prepared a place for you to stay."*

"What was this place?" asked Wilson.

"It was a cave, but we have expanded it over the years," Gaston replied.

They followed him past a pile of goods and there was what could only be described as a cosy nest hollowed out of the crates with cots set up for them to sleep on and rugs on the floor. Lanthorns provided light.

"We will come and get you when your boat arrives, and it is safe to board," Gaston said and left them.

"Well, this is nice," said Linnet in perfect English, surprising them as she had never used it before.

"A perfect home from home," said Wilson.

They settled in, blew out all the lanterns except one and went to sleep.

Marty's body clock woke him and when he checked his watch, he saw it was half past six in the morning. He had slept for four hours which was enough. The rest slept on, so he laid back down and thought about what they had been through so far and realised that they had been really lucky. *But,* he thought, *you make your own luck.*

He must have dozed off as the next thing he knew, he was being shaken awake and offered breakfast and a coffee. Rolland had made it by heating a pot over the burner of an oil lantern that had the glass removed. Ingenious!

They waited for what seemed ages but was only a matter of a few hours until Gaston returned and told them it was time to go. They expected to go back up to the mausoleum, but they were taken in the opposite direction and into a large tunnel. The floor stayed level for some time and then angled up until they reached a cavern which had a wooden ceiling.

Gaston reached above his head and knocked on the wood. There was an answering bang and Gaston moved them back down the tunnel a short way and extinguished the lantern. The ceiling pivoted down from the far end so that it formed a ramp when it touched the floor. They could see figures above and one called out a greeting to Gaston. He replied as he led them up into a boat shed. Once they were out, a team of men started taking crates down into the tunnel.

"They will be back with your cargo," Gaston explained. *"There is no point in wasting the chance to ship some goods. No?"*

Marty laughed and said, *"You people never miss a chance to make a Franc or two, do you?"*

Chapter 11: A Question of Honour

Marty and Armand sat in the office at the farm and had been going over what had happened in Amiens. Then Marty asked,

"What happened with the fishing boat you went to look for?"

"Ha, that was funny," Armand replied, Marty noticed that his pronunciation was getting better.

"We came upon a cutter smaller than ours with the fishing boat in tow. So, we showed our number and the identification signal and pulled up alongside. I went across and the lieutenant in charge, a Mister Crosby, wouldn't believe I was an officer of the British Navy and arrested me. He was even going to put me with the Deal boys in the cable locker," they both laughed at that.

"Well, at the sight of me being held at gunpoint our men ran out the guns and threatened to blow him out of the water. He went red in the face and started shouting that the bloody French wouldn't take 'is ship when his master took him to one side and said something to him. When he came back, he asked me to prove I was a British officer, so I pulled out my commission and the letter of protection and waved them under 'is nose."

"You mean these scoundrels are working on behalf of his majesty's government?" he cried, "whatever is the world coming to!"

"I then asked him to release all of the men and as they came up, I saw that the passenger from our first trip was amongst them. He told me that he needed to get to London as fast as possible, so we took 'im on the Snipe and sailed direct to London."

"Your first time up the Thames?" asked Marty.

"Oui. It is very tricky even in a small boat like a Cutter, I would not like to 'av to take the Alouette up it," Armand replied with a wry grin.

"Any idea what was so urgent that our friend had to get back so fast?" Marty asked

"Non, he said nothing. But whatever it was, he was very worried about something"

The next week or so went by in a routine sort of way. It was almost Christmas, so Marty planned to visit the de Marchets' then go to Dorset to visit his family as the weather wasn't suitable for sailing. So, he left two weeks before Christmas, hired a coach to take him to Canterbury. Once there he took the Post to London then a Hansom Cab to the de Marchets' house.

When he knocked on the impressive front door, he was immediately let in and taken to greet the family in the drawing room. The first thing he noticed was that Evelyn was absent, but he decided not to ask where she was. They were pleased to see him as usual and wanted to hear of his latest adventures. He had to be circumspect as officially most of what he had done came under the heading of clandestine, but he could talk about the cutting out of the Alouette. He was just finishing the tale when he heard the front door open and close and footsteps approach the door.

It opened and in walked Evelyn looking radiant with a blush that the cold air outside had brought to her fair skin. She saw Marty, and her mouth opened in a silent Oh, then a second figure came through the door and Marty understood. He was tall, fair-haired, handsome, and dressed in the uniform of the Lifeguards.

Evelyn gathered herself and said, "Marty! What a surprise! Arthur, you must meet Marty. You remember I told you about him?"

Arthur stepped forward and held out his hand, "Arthur Simmonds, Ensign, Lifeguards. Pleased to meet you."

Marty resisted the temptation to be rude and said, "Martin Stockley, midshipman, Royal Navy, delighted," and shook his hand firmly.

The two were similar in age and although Marty was shorter, he more than made up for that with his broad shoulders and powerful upper body developed by the years of climbing rigging and hauling on guns.

"Evelyn has told me about you and how you rescued the family from Toulon. I must say I am most envious, I haven't had a chance to see action yet as I've only been in the guards for four months."

That made Marty feel much better as compared to Arthur; he was a veteran.

The Count stepped in, "We are all attending a ball thrown by the Duchess of Devonshire tomorrow evening, and I am sure she would be pleased if you would join us. I will write her a note this afternoon."

Before Marty could respond, Evelyn said, "Oh my, we must get you some new clothes. You must look your best for that. All of London will be there!"

The Count laughed and said, "I am sure Martin will look perfectly well in uniform," and then to Marty, "You did bring your dress uniform, didn't you?"

Marty assured him he had.

The next evening saw him suited and booted in his best uniform. He wore his dirk but left his fighting knife, hanger and Nock pistols in his room. He did, however, slip a small 'barker' pocket pistol into his overcoat pocket as an insurance against footpads.

The whole family, minus their young son who wasn't old enough to attend, got into the family carriage and proceeded to Devonshire house.

It was huge and there was a queue of carriages waiting in line to unload their prestigious guests. They reached the front and disembarked. Marty was about to offer Evelyn his arm when he saw Arthur approaching and Evelyn's face light up in a smile as she saw him. Ruefully, he silently admitted to himself that any ideas he had about romance in that direction were history now.

They entered through the grand foyer and were announced. Marty was presented to the Duke and Duchess and followed the Count through the room. They stopped frequently, and he was introduced to a number of titled and very distinguished people. Then he came upon Admiral Hood.

"Martin, my boy!" He said in a voice that could have been heard at the top of the mainmast of the Victory. "What a pleasant surprise!"

Not bloody likely, thought Marty, *I bet the old fox knew exactly where I was*, but he smiled and bowed to the Admiral and said, "A flying visit to see the de Marchets family before heading down to Dorset, Sir."

"Splendid, splendid! We must have a talk before you leave," he said with a smile. He then leaned in conspiratorially and said in a low voice, "I see the Contessa is accounted for. But rather than try and repel boarders, I would look for another to cut out if I were you. It is, after all, a target rich environment." He winked at Marty and shooed him away. "Now run along and enjoy your evening."

Marty wandered through the crowd sipping a glass of white wine when Arthur found him and asked him to join a group that he and Evelyn were with. Seeing nothing better to do, Marty agreed and followed along.

The group was predominantly made up of young ladies, some of whom had their beaus with them and others that were, seemingly, single. To be honest, Marty found the talk rather tedious as it concerned scandal about people who he had never heard of or fashion which he knew nothing about either.

Then a rich, slightly husky voice said in his ear, "you don't look like you're having much fun." A shiver ran down his spine.

He looked around to see a beautiful face framed in auburn curls whose green eyes were looking boldly in to his. He turned and took a half-step back so he could see her better. She was about three inches shorter than him and dressed in a fashionable low-cut dress that showed off her slim waist and emphasised her breasts. He estimated she was older than him by a couple of years.

Evelyn stepped up beside him and said in a tight voice, "Hello, Lady Caroline. I didn't know you were attending the ball this evening."

"Why, Contessa Evelyn," the woman said with a beautiful smile, "it is so nice to see you!" Then she turned her eyes on Marty and said, "aren't you going to introduce me to your handsome friend?"

Marty didn't see Evelyn tense, nor did he hear the terse note in her voice as she replied, "Lady Caroline, may I introduce Midshipman Martin Stockley, a valued friend of my family."

"Not the heroic young man that rescued you from Toulon?" Caroline said and then focussing totally on Marty, she purred, "I would be fascinated to hear your telling of the story. We have heard so much about you."

And with that, she hooked her arm through his and led him away. Marty just heard Evelyn say, "*Well, really!*" in French as they moved into the crowd.

He was acutely aware of her body as they moved through the mass of people to the buffet. She moved with an effortless grace and seemed glued to his side. She released him once they were in front of the buffet table and started helping herself to morsels from the vast array of dishes.

"You must try the taurine of grouse with aspic," she said, "it's absolutely delightful."

He grinned at her and started filling a plate.

"Which ship are you on?" she asked.

"The Lark, Navy Cutter," he replied, giving the cover story. "We are based out of Deal and run messages to the channel fleet when we aren't training new men."

"Sounds fascinating," she said with a look that said it was anything but.

"I saw you talking with Admiral Lord Hood. You seem to be very well connected for one who 'runs messages'," and before he could respond, she leaned towards him, incidentally, offering him a wonderful view of her cleavage. "No matter. I am sure you have your secrets."

She smiled that devastating smile again and prompted him to tell the tale of Toulon. He was just getting to the part about going back for the Count's bag of valuables when an obviously inebriated man approached.

"Caroline, I have been looking everywhere for you," he looked down his nose at Marty, "what are you doing with this . . . sailor?" he said, "Come, let's go and dance," and he reached for her arm.

Lady Caroline gave him a look like she just trod on a dog turd and moved her arm away from him.

"Rufus," she said, "I told you I wouldn't be accompanying you tonight, or in fact ever again."

"You didn't mean it though, did you?" he said with despair then angrily, "You are mine!"

"I am no one's," she spat hotly, "*especially* not yours."

Marty stepped between them and said to the man,

"I don't think either of you want to cause a scene here in front of all these people."

He leaned in so he was face to face with Rufus and said, "So why don't you go away, sober up, and leave my lady in peace."

"YOUR LADY?" Rufus practically shouted, drawing the attention of everyone within earshot.

"YOUR LADY! I will kill you for that, you Navy scum," and with that he slapped Marty across the face.

"I will have satisfaction!" he cried, "my seconds will attend you directly."

With that, he turned and stalked off before Marty had a chance to react.

"Oh dear," Caroline said, grasping Marty's arm, "I am so sorry. I had no idea that fool would do that."

Then Arthur turned up, looking concerned.

"Marty, is it true? Are you to duel Rufus Arbuthnot?"

Marty looked slightly bemused and said,

"Well bad news travels fast, doesn't it? Yes, it would appear so. The man struck me for no reason!"

Caroline looked abashed at that and said,

"I am afraid it's my fault. I should have known that fool would strike out at anyone I was with after I pushed him away, and Martin was just trying to prevent a scene."

Arthur frowned at her and looked like he wanted to say something but thought better of it and instead said to Marty,

"I will act as your second with one of my brother officers. I will talk to Arbuthnot and try and get him to see sense." He walked off in the direction of the group.

Caroline laid her hand on Marty's arm and said,

"Martin, you must not fight him. He is an accomplished duellist and has killed at least three men."

Marty looked at her wondering how he had got onto this mess by just being nice to someone but said,

"Well, I've killed more than that, so we shall have to see, won't we."

Caroline looked surprised and he was about to say something else but he changed the subject asking her to dance.

The next morning, Marty had finished his breakfast and was talking with the Count about what had happened. The Count was rather ambivalent about the whole thing as duelling was common in France and was giving some unnecessary advice when they heard a knock on the front door. He looked up just as Arthur and another young officer walked in.

Arthur looked concerned and said,

"we tried to talk sense to the man, but he will not listen and so the duel is scheduled for dawn tomorrow morning on the heath at Hampstead."

Arthur then introduced the second officer as Wilson Spears, a fellow ensign in the Lifeguards.

"As the challenged, you can choose weapons," Wilson explained, "Arbuthnot is known to be an expert shot and a more than fair swordsman."

"Can I specify the type of weapon rather than just sword or pistol?" Marty asked.

"Yes, you can," Arthur answered.

"Then I choose hangers with a main gauche," Marty stated, "and the main gauche will be a fighting knife. I have one you can use as an example." And he produced the blade from its sheath in the small of his back.

The door burst open.

"YOU CANNOT DO THIS!" shouted Evelyn. "That woman is infamous. She married an older man and since he died, she has had one lover after another! She isn't worth dying over!"

"Well, you obviously think about as much of my fighting skills as you do her," Marty retorted offended.

"It's not about your skill," she said, calming down and heaving a big sigh, "It's about the cause. She isn't worth it."

"Oh! Well, don't worry. It's not about her," he said and smiled at the bemused look on her face, "that idiot hit me in public and whether she was there or not, I can't let that go."

Evelyn looked at Marty and then at Arthur and her father, who were all nodding in agreement.

"MEN!" she declared as she spun and left the room muttering and gesticulating.

The four of them looked at each other and Arthur said,

"Women will never understand us or our code of honour," the rest of them nodded sagely.

The next morning, Marty was up before dawn and dressed in a white silk shirt and tight fitting but flexible riding breeches. He wore hessian boots that were soft and supple and had ridged leather soles designed to be non-slip on a wet wooden deck. His long hair was tied back in a ponytail with a black ribbon and to finish it off, he wore black, fine calfskin gloves. If he had looked at himself in a mirror, he would have seen a handsome young man, well-muscled and proportioned, carrying a couple of scars from previous encounters and a confidence that belied his age.

Arthur and Wilson arrived on time and the three of them donned heavy cloaks before boarding one of the de Marchets' carriages that took them through the lamp-lit, slightly misty streets to Hampstead Heath. They arrived at the location to find another two carriages already there. Out of one, stepped Rufus and his seconds and out of the other, a man who Arthur identified as a surgeon with another who was the Master of Ceremonies.

Arthur and Wilson went to talk to Rufus's seconds. After a short exchange, they returned and told Marty,

"He won't listen to reason. The duel has to be fought."

Marty looked around and noticed two other carriages parked at the edge of the grassy area. *Who*, he wondered wryly, *would get up this early to watch a fight between two idiots with more honour than sense?*

Arthur led him to where a table had been set up, and he saw that there were two identical sets of weapons. Hunting hangers and long daggers. He had wanted fighting knives like his, but they couldn't find two identical ones at short notice. He examined them and decided these would do. They had nine to ten-inch blades that were sharp on both sides, a brass cross guard, and wooden handles wrapped in shagreen for better grip.

The master of ceremonies stepped up and said,

"The challenger may choose his weapons."

Rufus stepped forward, looked sneeringly at Marty, briefly examined both sets of weapons, and selected one. Marty took up the other.

"The contest will continue until one combatant can no longer compete," he announced.

"I will declare the winner when, in my judgment, one of you is no longer able to defend himself. Take your positions. Remember, you must break off the duel as soon as I call hold. If you do not, I will shoot you."

He pulled a duelling pistol from a pocket of his coat and pulled it to full cock.

The two of them went to the middle of the green and took up their fighting stances.

Rufus adopted a classic fencers poise with his main gauche held behind his back and his sword arm extended. His right leg forward of his body and flexed so his weight was more over it than the left.

Marty took more of a knife fighter's stance, slightly side-on with the hanger in the lead, feet shoulder-width apart and knees bent so his weight was evenly spread over the balls of his feet. Rufus frowned when he saw that as if not quite sure what to make of it.

The master of ceremonies stood to one side, half-way between them and levelled a long cane.

"Are you ready? Then En Garde!" The cane lifted out of the way.

Rufus shuffled forward in the classic fencing forward-step, and Marty let him come. He trusted his defence and speed of reaction to protect him.

Rufus feinted with a thrust to Marty's face, and Marty swatted it away with his main gauche and flicked his hanger at Rufus's waist.

Rufus jerked back out of range, and they settled again.

Marty swung a low attack with his hanger, causing Rufus to parry with his dagger and then launched a combination attack with both blades that caused a flurry of parries and ended with Rufus retreating in an arc to his left.

Rufus recovered and launched his own attack. High with the hanger followed by an uppercut with the dagger and then a sweeping slash to the waist with the hanger. Marty parried all three and spun away out of range to set again.

Marty was analysing his opponent and was sure he was being analysed too. There was another exchange, and he got a nick on his right bicep, which stung but didn't incapacitate him. He frowned. Something was nagging at him. Rufus launched another attack and the sword hissed passed Marty's face, and he noticed a brief frustrated look pass over his opponent's face. He realised that was supposed to be a killing stroke and Rufus had misjudged the range.

Marty suddenly realised Rufus wasn't used to fighting with a short blade!

He now knew how to win this. Fighters who used long blades tended to stay further apart and now Rufus would have to compensate by stepping in before he made a killing stroke. However, he had to end it quickly as he knew that Rufus would be adapting after every exchange.

He let Rufus launch an attack and backed up slowly, then, as he stepped back on his right foot, he appeared to slip and dropped to a knee. Rufus immediately pressed his attack with a long step forward on his left leg and launched an overhand attack with his sword. Marty didn't try and block it. Instead, he dived forward under the swing, knocking Rufus's dagger aside with his hanger and slicing across Rufus's extended left inner thigh with his own dagger. He rolled away to the right to complete the move and coincidently, avoided the spurt of blood from the severed femoral artery. He came smoothly to his feet to complete the move into guard.

He looked calmly at his opponent who had dropped both his blades and was frantically trying to stem the flow of blood from his leg.

The master of ceremonies called, "HOLD!" He and the surgeon rushed over and got Rufus to the ground, working frantically on him, but after just one minute, they stood and looked down at the still body in a pool of its own blood. The surgeon declared,

"He is dead; we could not stop the bleeding."

"You are the victor. Honour is satisfied," said the master of ceremonies.

Marty turned away and walked over to his seconds thinking, *What a bloody pointless waste.*

Wilson silently draped his cloak over his shoulders and Arthur took his weapons to return them to the table. He spoke to Rufus's seconds, shook hands with them then came back to where Marty stood.

"We can go now," he said.

He noticed that Marty's hands were as steady as a rock.

As they turned to go to their carriage, Marty looked over to the two that were parked nearby. He saw a silhouette appear at the window of one and in the morning sunlight, a beautiful face framed in auburn hair was revealed, smiled sadly and blew a kiss before disappearing into the shadows of the interior as the coach drove off.

Out of the other coach, stepped the Count and Admiral Hood, who came over and clasped his hand in turn.

"Never doubted you for a minute, m'boy," said the admiral.

"You fought with honour, mon cher," said the count, "I think it is time to celebrate."

They went to a chop house for breakfast that Arthur had booked in advance and were joined by Evelyn and her mother. Marty wasn't sure he wanted to eat, but the smell of the food soon overcame his reluctance and he wolfed down a man-sized portion.

He was still a teenager after all.

Chapter 12: Lost Innocence

"Did you have to kill him?" asked Caroline as they lay together in bed after a vigorous bout of lovemaking. Marty looked at her and wondered at the smoothness of her skin, which he could see quite a lot of as they were laying on top of the covers.

"I was taught that there is only one way to win a fight, and they drummed into me all the places you go for to finish it fast. I can't fight any other way."

She looked at him. At times, he looked his almost seventeen years with a sort of innocence in his face, but when she talked about his past or his life in the Navy, she saw the man he was, and part of that man was a killer and a leader. Confident, cool, and able.

He had told her about his early life in Dorset and being found by Captain Turner and his influence on him. He also talked about the other mentors he had had, John Batrick, the Cox, who had taught him to knife fight, Tom Savage, who had taught him so much about sailing, The Master, Mr. Trubshaw, who had taught him to Navigate, Mr. Evans, the Purser, who taught him to negotiate, and now Admiral Hood, Armand, and the Count de Marchets.

"Dead enemies don't follow you around," he grinned at her, "and I hate looking over my shoulder all the time."

She was nineteen years old, a widow and, although she was almost three years older, Marty was aware she was much more experienced than him in life and, particularly, in sex.

But, she thought wickedly, he was a fast learner.

He had received a note from her the day after the duel, inviting him to visit at her London house and the Count had encouraged him to do so. Evelyn had sniffed and put her nose in the air and refused to talk to him about her. He had taken her up on the invite and was now living there while he was in London.

Caroline had inherited a large fortune from her husband and had houses in London and Bath, an estate in Cheshire that covered three thousand acres or more and had enough tenants to populate a descent sized village. She was the youngest daughter of a merchant family and had been married to the much older Lord Candor for her family to gain some social advancement. He was the last of his line, and she had inherited his entire estate.

The rumour that the old boy had expired while 'in the saddle' were false as he had actually died of food poisoning after gorging himself on badly cooked Lampreys.

This made Lady Caroline the most eligible widow in Britain. However, she resented being treated like some kind of broodmare in waiting and she despised the fortune-seeking gadflies who constantly pursued her.

Marty, on the other hand, just accepted her as she was, made no demands, was good in bed (and getting better), was independently wealthy (to her surprise), and didn't have any interest in her fortune.

"You know I have to visit my family soon," he said, "Mum would never forgive me if I didn't go home for Christmas."

Her heart melted as she caught a glimpse of the young man behind the confident Naval officer in training.

"Of course, you must go," Caroline replied and started to twirl a lock of her hair around a finger, which Marty recognised as a sign she was thinking about something. "Would you mind if I came with you?" she suddenly asked. "I have nothing to keep me here and I don't want to be alone at Christmas either."

Marty thought that it must be hard to feel alone when you had a house full of servants but then he realised that like a Captain on a ship who had to be separate to his men, she couldn't be social with her servants.

"You know my people are common folk," he stated, "there aren't any servants down there."

She lifted he chin and said, "Do you think I can't manage without servants? My family weren't born into money either. We had little when I grew up."

Marty laughed and said,

"I meant nothing by it. I am sure you could survive anywhere." Then to distract her, he pulled her into a kiss which led to much more interesting things.

Two days later, they left in one of Caroline's coaches and headed towards Dorset. The weather was dry and very cold. They had heard that the Thames had frozen, people were skating on it, and they were talking about setting up a fair on the ice.

This made the trip faster albeit bumpier, but the expensive suspension on the coach made it relatively comfortable. They also found 'ways' to keep each other warm under the blankets that would scandalise the people they passed if they but knew.

They stopped at all the usual places to change horses and overnighted in Salisbury on the second night at the George Hotel in the centre of the City near to the Cathedral. From there, they changed horses in Blandford and arrived in Wareham after three days traveling.

They pulled up outside the Red Lion Hotel, and the landlord nearly fainted when he saw the crest on the coach. The aristocracy just didn't visit Wareham and they had never stayed at his hotel. He had his daughter act as maid of all works to her ladyship, and his wife, who Marty knew had as broad a Dorset accent as his mother, suddenly started speaking posh. Their son, who got the job of carrying the bags up to the room, looked at Marty who was dressed in fine civilian clothes curiously and then in astonishment.

"Marty?" he asked, "Be that you Marty Stockley?"

"Wondered when you would recognise me, Tim," he laughed, "It's been a while since we were at school together."

"I heard you was doin' all righ' mate, but I never though' you been and gone and hooked up with a real Lady. Do yer mum know?"

"Not yet, and I be thankful if yer would keep it under yer 'at," Marty said, letting his Dorset burr come out. "I wants to surprise 'er. Right?"

"Don't yer worry," replied Tim, "I'll keep er under me 'at. Mind you me mum will strain 'er throat if'n she don't stop talking funny." They both laughed at that.

Marty knew that in spite of the promise, in about an hour, most of Wareham would know that one of their own had come home with a real Lady in tow.

It was too late for them to visit that evening, so they settled down for the night and had a delicious meal of Jugged Steak, Dorset knobs, and Dorset apple cake.

The next morning, they set out, and Marty noticed that there were far more people loitering around the crossroads where the hotel was built than usual. He had to resist the temptation to wave as he recognised many of them.

They soon crossed the bridge over the Frome, and he saw a familiar blue and white painted barge tied up at the wharf. He smiled at the memory that evoked and looked around to see if he could see any of his old shipmates. They would visit with Miss Turner before they left, of course, and he hoped the captain would still be there.

They arrived at his mother's house. Marty thought of the house as his mother's even though he owned it, and, as the carriage drew up outside, he could hear the laughter of children playing and knew at least some of his brothers and sisters were there with their families.

He got out first and helped Caroline down the steps. She had dressed in a modest dress of sky blue with Dorset lace trim and looked absolutely beautiful. He opened the gate and stepped through when the front door burst open and his sister, Helen, ran out, jumped into his arms, wrapping her legs around his waist, yelling, "MARTY'S HOME."

Marty laughed and swung her around and was suddenly swamped with the rest of his brothers and sisters all wanting to get a hug in greeting. The crowd parted and there was his mum, still beautiful with grey in her hair and a smile on her face. She held out her arms, and he went to her and held her, surprised at how small she seemed to be.

She held him at arm's length and looked him up and down. "You've growed," she said and ran a hand over his cheek, "shavin' already too. You'm all growed up." She looked around him and said, "baint ye gonna introduce me to yer lady friend?"

Marty looked over his shoulder at Caroline, who still stood outside the gate smiling at him.

"Mum, everyone, I would like you to meet Caroline, my special friend. Caroline, this is my mum and my family." He took her by the hand and introduced to everyone in turn and finally to his mother.

"I am so pleased to meet you, Mrs. Stockley," Caroline greeted her, "Martin has told me so much about you."

"You cen call me Annie," said his mum with a brave attempt at speaking proper. "Now come on in afore ye freeze to death out here."

Inside, the adults sat in the living room, and the kids were banished to the parlour and kitchen. Marty had brought a box of wooden toys as presents, which he handed out to all the children before they were dismissed.

Annie looked at Caroline and said, "You must be a grand lady from the look of yer clothes and that carriage. You be a couple a year older than Marty?"

"And you want to know what my intentions are towards him?" said Caroline with a smile.

Marty looked at the two of them and decided this was one conversation he didn't want to get into the middle of.

Annie looked her straight in the eye and said,

"He be my youngest boy. He 'as six older brothers and two sisters, and I be seeing them married off to good partners and I will do the same for him."

Marty wanted the floor to open and swallow him up, but Caroline didn't bat an eyelid.

"Annie, I am a widow. I was married off at sixteen in an arranged marriage to an old man so my family could climb up a rung on the social ladder. He died a year ago and left me a sizeable fortune and a title that I don't give two hoots about. I have been chased like a fox by a pack of baying suitors who want to marry me for either my title or my money or both. Martin has never even asked about either and has even fought a duel (here Marty really cringed and tried to make himself as small as possible in his seat) to defend my honour. I am very fond of him and will grow to love him. Believe me, I will never hurt him."

Annie looked at Caroline and then at Marty, who was bright red and chuckled. "You'll do, me girl. You'll do."

Then she looked at Marty and said, "Don't you just sit there. Go and get us some tea!"

Marty practically fled to the kitchen where he met Helen wondering what the hell just happened.

"She be beautiful," said Helen.

"What?" said Marty coming out of his daze, "Oh yes, she is, and she is kind."

"Is she really a Lady. I mean, like Lady Banks?" Helen asked.

"Yes, she is Lady Candor, but she doesn't care much for the title," Marty replied.

"So, if you do marry her, you will be a Lord?"

Marty choked on the piece of lardy cake he was eating, and Helen hit him on the back a couple of times until he stopped coughing.

"Marry?" he eventually spluttered, "Blow me, I never even give that a thought!"

Helen was relentless, "But would you be a Lord if yous did?"

"I dunno, I suppose I could," he said, "but you be puttin' the cart afore the 'orse. We be jus' good friends."

"Yea right," Helen laughed, "Yer brothers were all married by eighteen."

They stayed for lunch and Marty had to tell everyone about his adventures again, which he did, though he left out any stories about his adventures in Kent.

He was pleased that his mother had a comfortable life now and that she could live happily on the money he was providing. He also talked to his next eldest brother, Arthur, who had left the mines and had spent the last four years working as an apprentice smith. He agreed to set him up with his own forge once he was qualified in a year's time.

They left the house an hour before dark and went back to the Red Lion. Marty tried hard not to think about what Helen had said, but he had to be honest with himself and admit that she had terrified him at the same time as starting him thinking.

The next day, they set off for Stoborough again but this time to visit Miss Taylor. They knocked at the door and Emily answered it. She didn't recognise him until he asked to see Miss Katy then she swept him up in a hug. A familiar voice came from behind her,

"Martin, my boy! How are you?" called Captain Taylor as he stepped out from the drawing room to see who the visitors were.

Emily stepped aside, and the two men shook hands.

"I am well, sir," Marty replied, "May I present Lady Caroline Candor."

"Delighted to meet you," Captain Taylor said as he bowed over the offered hand. Marty also noticed the appraising look he gave her and felt a protective pang of jealousy. Before he could react though, Miss Katy emerged from the parlour and bustled them all into the house. Once she had them all settled in the drawing room around the fire, she asked Emily to bring them tea.

Captain Taylor wanted to know what Marty had been up to since leaving the Falcon and was wise enough not to ask too many questions over the obvious (to him) omissions. He told Marty about their patrol which had carried on for months after he left the ship. They hadn't collected any more prizes and his biggest problem had been keeping the men occupied.

After Norway, they had returned to England for a refit, where he lost some of his men to some mysterious new unit, and then were attached to the Channel Fleet patrolling up and down the French coast. He did have one funny story about a revenue cutter who had hailed them, and the captain had come aboard the Falcon. The lieutenant was very cross and asked Captain Taylor if he was aware that there was a bunch of smugglers out of Deal who had the Admiralties protection. He looked at Marty directly with a raised eyebrow when he said that the lieutenant in charge of the Cutter that intervened on the smuggler's behalf was a Frenchman called Armand something or other.

Marty just smiled and asked how Cox John Batrick and Esi were. The captain accepted the change in subject as confirmation of his suspicions and told him that the cox was in Wareham with the crew of the barge. They were staying at the Row Barge Pub near the wharf. Esi was well and complaining as usual. He had found another cabin boy to help him, but Esi maintained 'he wasn't a patch on young Marty'.

In the meantime, Miss Kate had been chatting to Caroline and a peal of delighted laughter brought the men's attention back to the women.

"Were you really so small when you were here?" giggled Caroline.

Marty puffed up a bit in embarrassment and said he was just "a late developer."

Captain Taylor chipped in with a quip that he grew around three inches in the first six months on board and could eat enough to fuel two full grown topmen and still complain he was hungry.

Marty turned the conversation to the de Marchets telling that they were well and settled in London. Captain Taylor replied that he had the occasional letter from the count and that, in fact, he had one just recently.

"Oh?" said Marty, a little concerned about what was to come, "did he have any news?"

"He mentioned you had been in a duel and accounted for yourself well and with honour, if not a little unconventionally," replied Captain Turner.

"A duel?" cried Miss Kate, "You fought a duel?"

"Oops," said Turner, looking abashed at mentioning that in front of his sister who had very particular ideas about duelling and a number of other activities that young men partook in.

Fortunately, there was a knock at the front door and Emily rushed to answer it. A moment later, a Navy courier stepped into the drawing room.

Turner looked up expectantly, but the young man looked to Marty and said,

"Midshipman Stockley?"

Marty was surprised but said, "Yes?"

"I have orders for you," said the courier and handed him a packet with the fouled anchor seal of the admiralty.

"The landlord of the Red Lion said you would be here."

Marty signed the proffered receipt then cracked the seal and opened the letter inside. He read it carefully then said to the courier,

"Please convey my best wishes to Admiral Lord Hood and Mr. Wickham. Tell them I will leave immediately and expect to sail by the twenty-ninth, weather permitting."

He looked at Caroline and said,

"I am sorry, but I must leave immediately for Deal. A situation has arisen, and I am required to sail in the Lark as soon as possible."

Turner looked at him quizzically and said,

"A rum order for a 'training base' don't you think?"

Marty smiled and said,

"It seems Armand is injured and can't command her himself. The orders don't say why we need to sail."

Captain Turner just nodded and said thoughtfully,

"Hood and Wickham. Be careful, Martin, you are in dangerous company."

"Aye, aye, sir," said Marty with a smile, "but it's more fun than blockade duty."

Turner laughed and replied,

"true, but don't forget to keep up your studies for your lieutenants board. You will be able to sit it in a little over a year."

"I haven't forgotten, sir," Marty replied and shook Turner's hand. He kissed Miss Kate and asked her to tell his mother that he had been recalled and to give her his love.

Chapter 13: Puppy Love

When they got back to the hotel, Caroline started to pack her bags as well. When he looked at her quizzically, she said,

"You don't expect me to just let you swan off on your own do you? I will come to Deal and see you off when you leave."

The trip took three days, Marty had sent a message ahead by fast messenger for them to prepare the ship for sail so that when he arrived, they could set off immediately.

Armand had broken his leg when he slipped while getting out of a fishing boat and his leg dropped between the boat and the dock. They visited him at the farm and found him propped in a comfortable chair with his leg stuck out in front of him, splinted and bound tightly with a strip of cloth.

Marty introduced Caroline then excused himself as he had to get into uniform and get his sea chest packed. When he returned, he found the two of them laughing at a story that Armand was telling about Marty learning to ride. He entered the room with a grin and was about to say something witty when Caroline looked at him in shocked surprise. He stopped and said, "What?"

She recovered herself and said, "Oh, it's just I've never seen you with all your weapons before. You look so ………. Intimidating."

Marty looked down and realised that without thinking he had donned his full weapons harness with pistols, sword, and knife.

"Oh, this little number," he joked, "all the fashion in these parts y'know."

"Is that the infamous knife?" she asked.

He drew it.

She shuddered.

"It's monstrous," she said.

"It's effective," he replied and re-sheathed it.

Armand passed him a set of sealed orders that had 'Not to be opened until at sea' written under the seal.

There was nothing to delay him going to the ship now, although he was loath to leave Caroline, so he led the way to the dock. He stopped at the bottom of the gangway. She came into his arms and kissed him.

"Please be careful," she said, "I want to see you again."

"I will," he said.

She punched him on the arm and said, "Liar, don't make promises you won't keep. You will do what you have to as you always do. I will go to the London house. Let me know when you get back."

He grinned, kissed her on the nose, turned, and walked up the gangway to see all the crew and marines watching with big grins on their faces.

"What are you smiling at, you lubbers," he shouted, "Get this ship underway."

With that, he yelled the orders to cast off and get the ship out under sweeps into the channel.

He looked back just once and saw her still standing on the dock with a hand raised in farewell. He waved his hat then concentrated on getting them down the estuary and out to sea.

An hour later, they were well on their way and he went to his cabin to open the orders. They were signed by Wickham and not couched in the formal terms that the usual Navy orders were. They were explicit and to the point.

"So, it's Holland then," he said to himself and went immediately up on deck to give the master his orders.

Holland had become the Batavian Republic in 1795 when the French took over so was enemy territory. He was to make landfall South of the village of Noordwijk, which was between Amsterdam and The Hague where there was a long beach backed by dunes.

The weather was freezing cold and there was a good wind, but it wasn't snowing, so Marty thought they were lucky. They made good progress. According to his charts, they had to sail around one hundred- and sixty-miles Northwest to get to Noordwijk, then had to cruise South along the shore until they saw a signal light flashed four times short and three times long. The reply was two long and three short. Then he was to put ashore with a landing team and render whatever assistance the contact required.

"Detailed as usual," he muttered with deep irony.

He reasoned if they were to render assistance then they must be prepared for a trip in land. So, he would need fit men who were fast with a blade and a variety of 'other skills' to cover most situations. That was simple, he would take the Basques and Tom with Wilson and John Smith as back up in the boat party in case he needed them. The range of skills they had would cover most circumstances and their fighting ability was second to none. They would arrive on the coast on New Year's Eve.

They were on their second trip along the coast an hour or so after dusk when they saw the signal. Marty made the reply, ordered the ship heave to, and the boat alongside.

The oars were manned and the shore team ready to board. He inspected them one last time and made sure that they all had a pair of pistols that were loaded but not primed. Each man also carried the blade of his choice and a small pack containing food, a wooden flask of water, and spare ammunition. He had made sure they all wore sturdy shoes or boots with socks in anticipation of having to walk some distance ashore. He wore a pair of sturdy, calf length, lace-up boots normally worn by farmers. They were good for walking and he had hidden the blade of a cutthroat razor in the right boot upper and a pair of lockpicks in the left between the layers of leather.

Satisfied all was as ready as he could make it, he ordered the men to board. Last in, he got them under way and steered for the light. There was a slight swell and he noticed that there was a patch of breakers about halfway in, which he suspected was a sand bar just under the surface. He steered the boat around it just in case and then concentrated on keeping it straight as it came onto the surf up to the shore. The boat grounded on the gently shelving beach and the bow men jumped out and held it straight.

Marty was the first to jump from the bow to the sand and made his way to the figure standing with the now shielded lamp in his hand.

"Midshipman Martin Stockley," he said in introduction.

"Jeroen van Helden," replied the contact, "You have men to help?"

"Yes, but which ones depend on what you need help with," replied Marty.

"They haven't told you?" Jeroen said in surprise, "We must go to Scheveningen. There in the harbour is a boat, The Zeeland, on it are hidden the Stadholder's jewels. I guess in England you would call them the crown jewels. We need to board the ship and sail her out of the harbour to England. On our way there, we also need to rescue two former government ministers who are under house arrest on the outskirts of Den Haag."

"Oh" said Marty sarcastically "I was afraid it would be something really difficult. What type of boat are we to steal?"

"Not steal," Jeroen replied, "it's owned by one of the ministers. You just have to sail it. It's a yacht that was used for racing."

Marty turned to Tom and said, "We will need all of the boys. Send the boat back and tell them we will rendezvous off the port of Scheveningen South of here tomorrow night. If we don't show, they are to sail back to The Farm and we will see them there. It's too dangerous for them to hang around off this coast for too long."

Ten minutes later, they were following Jeroen along the beach heading South. He explained that there were five hundred meters of dunes behind the beach and it was easier just to walk along the firm shoreline. It was a clear night and very cold, but the stars shone brightly and gave ample light to walk by.

"Your English is very good. Where did you learn it?" Marty asked Jeroen.

"I was a trader and I would trade cheese and hemp mainly with England. I spent several weeks a year in Lowestoft and Great Yarmouth."

"Do we go all the way to Schevening on the beach?" asked Marty.

"Scheveningen," Jeroen corrected, "No, we need to go to Den Haag first and that is inland a little."

"Tell me about the house the ministers are being held in," said Marty.

The rest of the men closed in behind to listen in to the explanation.

"They are held in a lange boerderij. That is a long farmhouse where the people live in one end and the animals in the other. It is a very traditional Dutch building. The house is set a little back from the road with a vegetable garden in front. There are fields on either side and behind. In this one, there are fruit trees in the field to the right and they keep geese in the garden at the front. There is a dog, and she had a nest of pups two months ago. They are Hollandse Herders, a dog used to protect the farm animals and to keep the sheep on the dikes away from the crops. She will protect the farm and make noise if she sees you."

Marty wasn't pleased to hear that. He liked dogs and he didn't like the idea of having to silence one by killing it, especially if she had pups. He tried to think of another way.

They continued to walk along the beach in the starlight until they saw the outline of houses which Jeroen identified as the outskirts of Scheveningen. They turned off the beach on a track through the dunes and headed inland for around three miles.

Jeroen stopped them in a wooded area and whispered,

"The house is about one hundred meters ahead on the right."

They sent Antton ahead and he was only gone for a few minutes when he returned.

"There are no guards visible but there are four horses with what look like military saddles tied up outside and from the look of them they haven't been there long. The house is dark except for a light at the far left-hand end. I saw nothing of the dog but there are two geese roosting in a small hut in the garden. There is smoke coming from the chimney, so they have a fire going," he reported.

Marty thought for a minute then gave the men their orders.

Pablo, John, and Matai made their way through the trees to get around behind the house where Jeroen said there would be a large stack of wood up against the back wall. The rest made their way up the track to the front.

Marty got the men spread out along the low wall that separated the property from the road and they waited. It got even colder, and he was sure there was a frost setting in. Then he saw a movement on the roof. He was hoping the thatch would muffle the sound as someone climbed up from the back of the house to the chimney.

The figure got to the chimney then stuffed something in it blocking off the smoke. He then sat down on the ridge and waited.

A few minutes later, there was a shout from inside the house followed by a lot of coughing. The front door burst open and people started to come out in a cloud of smoke. Marty's men moved in during the confusion and while the former occupants were still suffering from streaming eyes and coughing, quickly subdued them and tied them up.

Around the same time as the door burst open, a fierce barking from the other end of the building started accompanied by shrill yips and high-pitched barks that could only come from the puppies that Jeroen had mentioned. Marty had anticipated that and got Antton to make sure the door to the stable was barred. The dog could bark all it wanted now.

Once they were sure they had everyone secured, Marty signalled the man on the roof, who turned out to be Pablo, to unblock the chimney. Jeroen went to each person in turn and untied two with some rapid-fire Dutch obviously intended to placate them.

The three came through the house from the back with a large, formidable woman in tow. John Smith was holding his eye, and the two Basques were laughing so hard they were having a hard time walking. Marty scowled at them and Pablo explained in French that the woman had come out of the house, John had moved into restrain her only to be met with one of the best right hooks Pablo had ever seen that put John on his backside on the floor. The two Basques then took steps to calm the woman and assure her they meant her no harm.

The dog was still barking and sounded like it was getting angrier. Marty grabbed Jeroen's arm and said,

"We need to shut that dog up before it rouses the whole district."

Jeroen turned to the old lady and spoke to her. She nodded and took Marty by the arm, leading him to the door to the stable. She looked him in the eyes and made a shush for him to be quiet then she opened the door and out flew a brindled tornado! It was wolf shaped and around the size of a large collie. It greeted the old lady by running around her and then going up on its back legs, placing its paws on her chest and licking her chin vigorously. It was followed by eleven miniature versions of itself. Some stood back from Marty and yipped at him with high-pitched barks, others sniffed his boots and one got up on its back legs and put its paws on his leg.

On impulse, he reached down and picked it up and cradled it in his arms. The pup, a boy he could clearly see, stretched out its neck and managed to lick him under the chin. He raised it up a little so it could reach him easier and it snuggled into his neck and licked him some more.

The old lady looked at him then the pup. She smiled, putting her hand on the pup looked directly into Marty's eyes and nodded.

What does that mean? thought Marty, and he looked around to see Jeroen watching with a smile on his face.

The old woman said something to Jeroen and gestured at Marty. "She says the pup has chosen you. You must take it with you."

"What?" said Marty, "How can I …." Then he felt another lick and looking down into a pair of deep brown eyes, and was lost.

He dragged himself back to the now. The soldiers who were supposed to be guarding the ministers were trussed up and propped by the door. The old lady was talking to the two ministers who were now dressed in coats and hats and had bags with their necessities ready to travel.

"Get those men inside and make sure their bonds are secure," he ordered in French. He then addressed the two elderly men.

"Do either of you speak English or French?"

The younger of the two replied in English.

"I speak a little English, but my colleague only speaks Dutch."

"We need to get to Scheveningen before first light, so we need to leave now. Are you ready?"

"We are, but it would be better if my friend could ride on one of those horses. He has arthrosis and Scheveningen is too far for him to walk."

Marty ordered the horses to be brought over, got the men mounted, and told Tom and John to take the other two. He then realised he was still holding the pup and decided the best way to carry it was inside his coat. Jeroen was watching and grinned at him. The old lady came to him, stroked the puppies head, gave Marty a bag and said something to Jeroen.

"She says that you must make the pup your friend and he will protect you with his life. There is food for him in the bag." Jeroen translated.

She said something else.

"She said to feed the dog with your eyes. She means don't let him get fat. They are best kept skinny and well-exercised."

"What is thank you in Dutch?" Marty asked.

"Hartelijk dank," said Jeroen.

Marty looked the women in the eyes and said,

"Hartelijk dank for the pup," then leaned forward and kissed her on the cheek.

She laughed and kissed him three times alternately on each cheek.

It was Jeroen's turn to laugh as he told Marty that three kisses were the norm in Holland.

As they set off back down the road, Marty asked Jeroen.

"What are these dogs like to own?"

"Loyal, protective, brave, and love to work," Jeroen replied. "They are used for everything from herding sheep to guard dogs and police work."

Marty thought for a while and then asked,

"How big will he grow? He is a stocky little fellow right now, but his mother was, what, around fifty to fifty-five pounds?"

"The males get bigger," Jeroen laughed, "He could get to thirty-five Kilos that's around seventy-five pounds."

"Oh, quite big then," Marty said in wonder as the pup was fast asleep in his cocoon in Marty's coat and having a dream snuffling and moving his legs as he relived some adventure he had during the day. It weighed just twelve pounds at the time.

"When do they get to full size?'

"Oh, at around two and a half to three years old. They grow tall for the first year or so and then put on muscle for the next eighteen months to two years. They live quite long lives for dogs, and some get to fourteen years!" Jeroen told him. "They are also very intelligent and easily trained. Just use lots of food as bribes."

They walked on and Marty noticed some low clouds scudding across the sky from the West. If the wind at sea level was the same, they would have trouble leaving harbour.

They entered the outskirts of Scheveningen at around four in the morning. The men became more alert as they started to pass houses and the noise of the horses walking sounded preternaturally loud. But no lights came on and apart from the odd woof from an inquisitive dog and cats running across the road on their nocturnal patrols they saw no one.

They reached the harbour and Jeroen pointed out the yacht. She was a beauty, moored to a buoy in the centre of the harbour, she rode high in the water. Single-masted and gaff-rigged with a typically Dutch hull with lee boards and raised poop deck.

They borrowed a rowboat to ferry them across. He saw the yacht was called the Anika, and once on, he started a quick inventory of what was aboard. There was a cabin and he put the now wide-awake pup in there while he searched it. He discovered then that pups have no bladder control as it immediately peed on the deck. So, he mopped it up with a rag and gave him some water and a bit of sausage he had in his pack.

One thing became clear almost immediately. The boat hadn't been stocked with food or water. Food they could do without as they still had some of their rations left over but water was something they couldn't miss. So, he sent Matai and Jeroen ashore to find a pump to fill a couple of barricos with water, then turned his attention to the sails and rigging. The Anika was well found with serviceable rigging and two sets of sails, neither of which were rigged. He decided that it would be fastest to set up the lighter weight set and put the boys to work.

While they were busy rigging the sails, he studied the exit from the harbour. The channel ran Northwest and according to the chart, there were sand bars close in shore that they would have to avoid. With her fore and aft sails, she should be able to negotiate that with a Westerly breeze blowing.

A bump announced the return of Matai and Jeroen and he went over to help them get the kegs on board. Matai passed up a large flour sack. Curious, Marty opened it and saw a couple of round cheeses, several loaves of bread, and long dried sausages. He decided he didn't want to know where that had come from and to just be grateful for breakfast.

"The sails be all rigged, Sir," Tom reported. "We be ready for sea whenever you wants to leave."

"OK, set the foresail and let go the mooring. Let's see how she behaves," said Marty and moved to take the tiller.

Up went the foresail and as it filled, the men let go one end of the cable that was looped through the mooring ring on the buoy.

"Brace up," called Marty and the crew pulled on the lines that trimmed the sail taught so the wind blew along the length of it. They started to make headway and Marty felt the rudder bite. He made sure he knew where the landmarks were that he needed to steer by to find the exit and sent Tom to the bow to signal any slight changes of course he needed to make.

There was a shout from the shore. Marty looked back and was surprised to see the glow of the dawn sun coming over the horizon. He couldn't see who shouted or what was said but there was a flash then a bang and a musket ball hissed by over his head. Marty guessed that the guards at the farm had gotten free and had run to Scheveningen to raise the alarm.

To get out of the harbour, they had to pass through a narrow entrance before running the channel through the beach. If the Dutch soldiers managed to get enough men at the harbour mouth, they would have to run a gauntlet of musket fire at the least.

With such a light breeze and only the foresail set, they were creeping along at around two to three knots. He didn't want to go any faster in the near dark as he had to "feel" his way through the exit. Another couple of shots rang out from the larboard side and one ricocheted of the rail and missed him by a foot or so.

Bugger this is getting warm, he thought.

He glanced back at the Eastern horizon. The sun was just showing its upper rim. He looked to larboard and realized he could see the shoreline and around a dozen soldiers running to get to the Southern arm of the harbour mouth before them.

"Haul the mainsail!" he shouted, deciding the time for caution was gone. His men rushed to obey and hauled the gaff boom up with the sail attached to it. It stopped half-way up. The ring around the mast that attached to the top boom had twisted and jammed. He saw Antton climbing up to try and stamp it free.

There was a volley of shots, and Antton grabbed at his side. He lost his hold and fell but Wilson came out of nowhere to catch the much smaller man and lower him to the deck. He took Antton's place and hauled himself up a rope to where he could stamp down on the ring to try and free it.

Another volley. Marty looked across and could see the soldiers had reached the harbour mouth and were stood in a row reloading their muskets.

He would have given anything at that moment for a single carronade, but the yacht was unarmed.

Wish we had some muskets even, he thought to himself.

There was a loud clank, and the sail started up the mast again. Wilson dropped to the deck and joined the men hauling.

Another volley and bullets whizzed past like angry hornets, biting chunks out of the woodwork and tugging at the rigging.

They were accelerating, almost up to five knots he estimated.

Christ more of them, he thought as he watched another troop of soldiers arrive on the point and form up into a second rank. *They are going to wait till we are in the harbour mouth and they can't miss from that range.*

They entered the harbour mouth with their bowsprit just level with the wall. Marty braced himself and yelled,

"Everybody DOWN!"

The entire crew went flat to the deck. Marty crouched as low as he could while still being able to steer.

It was like the world held its breath and everything shifted into slow motion. The soldiers let go with another volley and the bullets buzzed angrily past over his head. The smoke from their guns obscuring them.

There was a second volley that buzzed angrily through the rigging. It was aimed slightly high.

"The smoke is blinding them," he said to John who stood close by.

"We have a chance!"

In defiance of the soldiers and without any hope of hitting them, he pulled out one of his pistols and shot it in their direction. Then he saw that their stern was clearing the exit and they were passing through the beach.

Marty was about to shout another warning when there was the Chuff-Boom of a small broadside of carronades. The ground around the soldiers erupted in geysers of sand and dirt as balls struck home. When the dust settled moments later, he saw that the two ranks had been decimated by a hail of cannister shot.

"Tis the Lark!" shouted Tom from the foredeck.

Marty stood and looked forward. There, with the rising sun shining on her sails, rode the Lark with the men lining the side waving like mad things and yelling their heads off.

A half hour later, the two craft were heading South West on course to the Thames Estuary and Chatham where Marty's orders told him to deliver the yacht, it's cargo, and the ministers.

He left the tiller to John and went below to check on the ministers and his pup. He found all three in the cabin. The ministers sat comfortably on the benches along the hull and the pup curled up asleep under the table. Antton was propped in a corner with his chest bandaged where the musket ball had dug a farrow as it skidded along his ribs. But apart from losing a drop or two of blood, he was sore rather than disabled. They had left Jeroen on shore as he said he still had work to do.

He greeted the men and at the sound of his voice, the pup got to its feet and trotted over to him. He picked it up and it snuggled its head under his chin and washed his neck with its little soft tongue.

"Are you well?" he asked the ministers.

"Ya alles goed," the older one replied with the characteristic Dutch GGGHHH at the start of good.

"Martyn van Boekel," he added, introducing himself and holding out his hand.

Marty shook it and replied, "Pleasure to meet you, sir."

The other man held out his hand and said in good English, "I am Artur van Grinsven. We would like to thank you and your men for rescuing us and our countries treasures. It would have been very bad if the French got their hands on it. They are robbing us blind with extortionate war reparation taxes as it is."

"Our honour to help you, sir," Marty replied.

Van Grinsven looked at him more closely and he said in surprise, "My God, you are just a jounger! How old are you, my boy?"

Marty bristled a bit at that.

"Seventeen, sir, and five years in the service of his majesty's Navy. Now, second in command of the unit tasked with this operation," he replied a little sharply.

"Oh, I meant no insult," van Grinsven smiled, "You are obviously capable and Mijnheer Wickham must have much faith in you."

"None taken, sir."

The pup chose that moment to whine and wiggle in his arms.

"He will be a fine dog when he is older," said van Grinsven, "But I think he needs to be fed and given a drink right now and you might want to clean up the little present he left under the table," he added with a smile.

Chapter 14: Undercover Jinx

Marty was back at the farm playing with, Blaez, his pup. According to Armand, Blaez was "wolf" in old Breton, and Marty reckoned that it was a very apt name for his new best friend. They were enjoying a game of tug that soon dissolved into a mini wrestling match as the pup decided it was more fun to jump on Marty's hands than the toy. Marty enjoyed it but, damn the pup's teeth were as sharp as needles! It was the end of January, and it was a snowy winter, so they were stuck playing in doors. What amazed him was how fast the pup was growing!

He heard a horse come up the gravel drive and stop outside the front door and then a loud knock. Will Barbour, their servant, went to the door and opened it. Blaez set himself foursquare in front of Marty and barked with the hair on his back raised up.

"Steady boy," Marty said as he stood. The pup looked over his shoulder at him and quieted but kept his attention on the door.

There was a knock and it opened. Will led in a Navy courier who was still shaking snow from his cloak.

"Midshipman Stockley?" he asked. When Marty nodded, he reached into his bag and took out two packages. One looked like it was a standard set of orders, but the other was much bulkier.

"These are from Admiral Hood," he held out a receipt pad, "Can you sign that you have received them."

Marty thanked him and signed where the man indicated.

"Would you like some food before you return?" Marty asked.

"I am to wait for your reply once you have read your orders," he replied, "so I would be grateful to get warm, dry out a bit, and get something to eat."

"Will, please take our friend here to the kitchen and take care of him," Marty asked.

He took the packages into the office and slit open the orders first. He read them and then sat back with his eyebrows raised in surprise. The door opened, and Armand came in. He was still limping from his broken leg and was using a cane to help him walk. He looked at Marty's face and said,

"What is it?"

"Well, I think we just found out what had our friend so agitated when you rescued him from the excise," Marty told him.

"It would appear the French are planning something for their fleet and a very large army out of Toulon and our friend wants to know what they are up to. He wants me to go to Toulon as soon as possible, assess the forces and ships, and find out whatever I can. There will be another agent joining us before we sail."

"I will get the Alouette prepared to leave immediately," Armand said.

"Thank you," Marty replied.

He didn't need to ask if Armand was fit enough to command her. He couldn't stop him if he wanted to. He took out a paper and picked up a pen and wrote a short reply for Hood and Wickham. He then called Will and wrote a second note while he waited for him to arrive.

"Can you get this message to Bill Clarence as soon as possible?" he said, handing him the sealed envelope.

In it, he was informing him that they would be away for a while. He asked him to send the boys over that normally crewed the Alouette and for them to be prepared to be away for an extended trip. He knew that Bill wouldn't ask why or where, and he'd trust that whatever they were up to would bring a profit one way or another. He also gave Will the envelope for the courier to take back to the Admiralty.

He then opened the second package. It contained a report of everything the agent had been able to discover. Reports of overheard conversations between ministers, the minutes of a meeting of the supply board, and a copy of a map of Toulon showing where the staging areas for troops and supplies were.

Plenty of time to read all that on the voyage to Toulon, he thought.

He picked a fresh piece of blank paper and wrote a letter to Caroline. He told her he had orders to sail and would be away for a while, but he would see her as soon as he returned and for her not to worry. He knew that wouldn't satisfy her and that she would corner Hood as soon as she could to try and get the where and why out of him, but that was Hood's problem to deal with.

He then went to the closet where they stored clothes that were useful for traveling in France and selected a couple of sets that he thought might be useful and packed them in his sea trunk.

He then checked over a pair of half inch calibre, eight-inch, double barrelled pistols he bought last time in London. They had the new rifling and were accurate up to about twenty-five yards. They were easier to conceal than his Nocks and gave him almost as much fire power. The gunsmith who made them was young and not afraid to experiment with new techniques. He put them back in their box, which had a powder flask, balls and ball mould as well as a cleaning kit, oil, and spare flints.

The box went into the chest along with a set of throwing knives, a pair of punch daggers, and two stilettoes. He then packed his personal kit, which now included a razor and finally his uniforms that were all new from his last trip to London, as he had outgrown all his old ones.

He checked his watch. It was time for dinner, and he knew that the Alouette wouldn't be ready to sail until at least the next afternoon's tide. He was one month off his seventeenth birthday and the thought of missing a meal could cause him physical pain.

Armand returned in time to sit down with the men in the common dining room that they shared with the master and mates when ashore. It wasn't conventional, but it was convenient. Will had gotten the cook to prepare a special meal as he knew they would all be leaving the next day. They had one of Marty's favourites, faggots. These were rich meat balls of pork liver, belly, and lights (heart, lungs, and kidneys), onions and sage wrapped in a caul and baked in gravy in the oven, along with a steak and onion pie, mashed and boiled potatoes, roasted parsnips, mashed buttered swede and sprouts. Pudding was a spotted dick with custard or crème anglaise, as Armand called it.

They were just about to get stuck in when there was a knock on the front door. Will went out to see who it was. A minute later, the dining room door opened and in walked a woman in a deep blue cloak with the hood pulled up over her head concealing her face. As the men stood, she reached up and pulled the hood back to reveal blond hair and an elfin face.

"Linette!" Marty cried as she looked up.

"Hello Marty," she smiled and looked around the room. Her eyes rested on Wilson, she smiled and said,

"Hello Wilson, are you well?"

"Aye and even better for seein' you, Miss Linette."

"Are you the second agent for this trip?" Marty asked.

"Yes, but please continue your meal."

Armand, who had never seen Linette, couldn't take his eyes off her and told Will to get her a chair so she could eat with them.

She looked at the food on the table with interest and said,

"The meatballs, are they the West Country faggots?" Arnaud replied that they were, and they were a speciality of the cook who came from Wiltshire.

Linette took two with some potatoes and sprouts and tucked in. The men laughed and got stuck into their own meal.

After dinner, Marty, Armand, and Linette sat down in front of the fire and talked about the upcoming mission.

"Wickham thought it would be easier to move around if we had a convincing cover story," she told them.

"You are old enough now to be in the Army in France and we need a reason why you have not been conscripted."

"Wait a minute," said Marty, "wouldn't it be easier if I was in the Army to get the information we need?"

"Only if you were in the supply corps," replied Linette dismissively.

"We will have the cover story that we are representatives of the committee checking on the deployment of the army and supplies."

"Won't that be easy to check?" said Armand.

"Yes, we want it to be because they will find that there is in fact a two-person team that has been sent from Paris and they will be Mademoiselle Antoinette Riccard and her colleague Philippe Dominique who work for the Ministries of war and supply respectively. The orders for the two have been carefully placed in both the Ministries files. Signed by the minister of war himself."

"How on earth did you manage that?" Marty asked in astonishment.

"Your friend whom you brought back to England before Christmas. The one you," she nodded at Armand, "rescued from the Revenue cutter. He returned to France and at great risk to himself, planted the orders in the file. The signatures are genuine as well." She gave a coy smile that told them not to ask how that had been achieved.

"So, how long has this mission been in planning then?" said Marty.

"Since he returned to England with the initial information," she replied.

"Damn, and I only got involved today," Marty exclaimed.

"You were always involved," Linette smiled, "Wickham was most insistent that you be the one that was sent along with me."

"I don't think any of my clothes are suitable for this part," Marty said after thinking over the cover story for a minute or two.

"Do not worry. I have several sets of clothes in my trunks for you. We checked with your tailor for your size, so they should all fit perfectly," she said with an arch look that teased about how much Wickham and his organisation knew about him.

Not to be out done, Marty said, "Shoes too?"

"Of course," Linette replied with a chuckle, "and boots with your special modifications as well."

"Modifications?" asked Armand in surprise.

"That will be the hidden blade from a razor stitched into the leg of the boot," Marty replied.

"And the extra strong laces, and lockpicks" added Linette.

"Damn it, is there nothing Wickham doesn't know," Marty muttered in irritation.

"Nothing that matters," replied Linette with a smile.

The next morning, they had a good breakfast with just the usual on offer, lamb chops, devilled kidneys, bacon, kippers, sausages, fried and scrambled eggs, toast, coffee, tea, jam, and marmalade. Linette ate some toast and marmalade. The boys fuelled up. Tom came in and told them that the Deal boys had arrived and had boarded the Alouette.

The tide was coming in and would peak at just after noon, so they would set sail on the ebb. Tom helped himself to breakfast while the others got themselves and their sea chests out of the farm onto the cart that took them to the dock.

Marty left Blaez with Will with instructions for feeding and exercise. He hated to leave him behind, but he was too young to accompany them on this mission.

They settled in quickly. Armand gave up half his cabin for Linette and Marty had the first lieutenants cabin as he usually did when Armand was on board. The crew had partitioned the cabin so that she had the use of the private head, so Armand had to use the heads at the bow like the rest of the crew, much to his dismay. It was cold hanging over the water and his healing leg made it slightly hazardous!

They planned to stop over at Gibraltar to restock and top up the water before the final run up to Toulon. The Alouette would stay nearby while the two 'agents' were in place, so they wanted to have maximum endurance.

To enable regular contact Armand would come ashore via the fishing village of Sanary that was just to the West of Toulon. He would make his way to a particular Café in the Toulon harbour district where he could pick up messages dropped by Marty without actually meeting him face to face.

Marty would be at the café at a particular time on a particular day. He would read a copy of Le Monitor. Once he spotted Armand, he would leave his table with the paper left on the seat. Armand would move in on the table and buy a coffee. When he left, he would just take the paper with him. The message would be encoded in the paper itself by pin pricks below the letters that made it up. By holding up the pages to the light, Armand could retrieve the message letter by letter. Anybody else who picked up the paper wouldn't notice the pin pricks or if they did, they wouldn't understand their significance.

It was late January and the trip down was beset by storms and contrary winds. It was so bad it took them three weeks to get to Gibraltar. They restocked and watered in two days and headed out into the Mediterranean towards the East. Their luck changed and they had a stiff South-westerly wind to drive them along at a good eleven knots. The Swan changed back into The Alouette and flew the French tricolour.

Their cover story had them travelling from Paris via Lyon down to Marseilles and then to Toulon. They would land close to where Marty landed with Armand when they had infiltrated Marseilles, make their way into the town and rent or buy a carriage to take them to Toulon. They spent every minute perfecting their new personas as they knew their lives depended on them being very convincing.

They arrived in good time, which made up a little for the delay in getting to Gibraltar and the landing went smoothly. The walk into Marseilles was chilly but the exercise kept them warm. They planned to stay in the town for a couple of days to fix their trail there, so they found a hotel frequented by government officials and set about establishing their identities.

They got lucky. No one there was from Paris and the fact that they were kept most people at arm's length. After two days, they rented a carriage and set off for Toulon. It was about fifty miles, so they stopped to change horses at La Ciotat and have some lunch. They arrived in Toulon just before dark, checked into a hotel that had been chosen specifically because it was frequented by Army officers and where Linette could use her charms to gather information.

Dressed in the austere black suit and hat that was the de-rigour dress of government employees, Marty actually looked much older than his seventeen years. He had a leather document bag with the seal of the ministry of supply embossed on the flap in which he had fake ledgers and letters of lading. Linette had a similar bag with the seal of the ministry of war.

They stayed strictly in character, only using their cover names and speaking French at all times. They assumed an arrogance that only government officials have and didn't hesitate to be demanding of people they came across.

They were, however, underneath it all, very nervous. They were, after all, at a major French Navy port that was also being used to stage a huge army and the supplies required for an important expedition. There were not only the military police but also the civil and secret police to contend with. One slip and they would be undone.

They decided the first thing they needed to do was establish exactly what ships were assembled to transport the army. So, they took a walk up to one of the forts that overlooked Toulon Harbour and started making notes. Now, they knew if they were caught with notes about things that didn't concern their characters, they would have uncomfortable questions to answer, so they had come up with a substitute code.

1 x nnn x n = 1st rate x nnn guns x number of

2 x nnn x n = 2nd rate x nnn guns x number of

And so on for ships of war and

T x nnnnnnn x n = Troop ship x tonnage x number of

HT x nnnnnnn x n = Horse Transport x tonnage x number of

And so on for all the different types of transport. They didn't make lists. Instead, they embedded the numbers in other documents, seemingly randomly, to hide them. They counted ten ships of the line including the massive L'Orient and two frigates. They knew that ships would come and go but these were sitting with yards crossed and looked to be unprepared for immediate departure.

There weren't many transports, but that wasn't a surprise as you would expect transports to arrive just before they were needed.

Having done that, they moved on to checking out the supplies. There wasn't much there yet, but the army had laid out areas where they would be stored, and it was very impressive. They were also setting up assembly areas for troops and artillery and stabling for cavalry mounts and draft horses. They marked them all on a map and would revisit them regularly.

The first message drop day was approaching, so they prepared the message and encoded it in a week-old newspaper. They used an out-of-date edition as that was less likely to be picked up by a stranger.

Marty was at the café at the time allocated for that pickup day. The time varied from drop to drop so no one could pick up on a routine. He waited and drank his coffee slowly, and when he saw Armand wandering into the square and up to the café, he finished his coffee and stood to leave, dropping the paper on to the seat of the chair he had been sat on. He wandered off without looking at Armand at all, which was hard.

Armand saw Marty get up and leave. The drop of the paper was done so well he didn't even see him do it. He walked up slowly and took a seat at the same table. There was the paper on the seat Marty just left. Job done.

A few days later, Marty and Linette met up as usual in her room to review what they had found. Their next drop to Armand was due in two days and they had woefully little information for him. The build-up of supplies was progressing slowly. An Artillery brigade had arrived and set up camp in one the pre-designated areas. There was no sense of urgency.

"We need to find out something more concrete," Linette sighed, *"I think it's time I tried working one of the officers."*

"Which one?" Marty asked, *"There are two or three that would love to get you into bed."*

"Pheh! None of them are worth the trouble," she said scornfully, *"I had in mind that colonel from the Infantry. The one with the braids and spectacular moustache."*

"Ha! I would have more luck with him! He prefers boys," Marty laughed.

"Then the dashing Commandant of Grenadiers who is on the central staff," she suggested, also laughing.

"Hmm yes, he would do," Marty said thoughtfully, *"He carries around that document case all the time. I wonder what's in it other than a saucisson."*

The next evening, Linette found the commandant sitting at a table in the café next to their hotel slurping down a bowl of onion soup. She made a play of looking around then approached him and asked if she could share his table. He stood up so fast, he nearly tipped the table over and bowed deeply to her.

"Certainly! My pleasure madam," he all but crooned.

"Mademoiselle," she said, batting her eyelids, *"Antoinette Riccard,"* she held out her hand.

"You are with the ministry of war, I believe," he said as he bowed over it.

"Why, yes I am," she replied as if surprised that she was worthy of such notice. She sat, and he followed suit.

He offered her a glass of wine, which she accepted and then called over a waiter. She ordered Bouillabaisse and some bread.

She let him serve her more wine as they sat and chatted. Marty was watching from another Café just down the road while he had a dinner of Duck liver and salad. Marty knew that despite her slim build, Linette had a prodigious capacity for wine. He had never seen her drunk even after a couple of bottles.

The same could not be said for the commandant, who after a bottle, was noticeably wobbly. Linette got another bottle from the waiter and two glasses and after they had drunk half of it, led the slurring and staggering man to her room. He just about made it to the chair by the bed and plopped himself down. Linette fed him another glass of wine while sitting on his lap and then his head lolled back, and he started to snore.

She went to the door and opened it. Marty was leaning on the wall opposite and immediately made his way into the room.

"Didn't take much to get him soused," he said.

"Aah, but he was drinking far more than he thought," said Linette and took a small flask out of her sleeve. She offered it to Marty and he took out the stopper and sniffed it.

"That's raw spirit!" he said as his eyes watered.

"Yes, almost pure alcohol," smirked Linette. *"I slipped some into most of the glasses he drank."*

"Poor bastard is going to have a hell of a headache in the morning," laughed Marty.

The commandant's bag laid on the floor next to him. It was locked but that didn't hold Marty up for more than a few seconds. He carefully removed the papers from inside making sure he noted in what order they were in. He then settled down to read them. Most were just memos between departments of the staff, but some were copies of orders that had been sent to the commanders of various units. One stood out above the rest. It was to the commander of the Army of Italy and ordered him to send five thousand troops to Genoa for embarkment on to ships by the beginning of April. Marty copied it and returned it to its correct place in the stack.

"What are they up to?" Marty mused. *"A formidable fleet and looking at the prepared staging areas at least twenty thousand men in Toulon plus the five thousand from Genoa."*

Lisette went to her valise and took out a small bottle, which she uncorked and held under the commandant's nose. Marty picked up a whiff of ammonia and identified it as smelling salts. The commandant coughed as the acrid fumes registered on his alcohol sodden brain. He opened his eyes and Linette sat on his lap and cradled his head.

"Where are the soldiers going?" she asked.

He just rolled his eyes up into his head and passed out again.

"You will get more out of a corpse," Marty scoffed.

Just then, the commandant jerked awake and slurred, *"Nobody knows. My god, they tell us nothing. Only Napoleon,"* and promptly passed out again.

There was a knock on the door. They looked at each other, and Linette pointed to the bed. Marty crawled under it and stayed very still.

She opened the door. There was an army officer outside.

"Can I help you?" she asked.

"Good evening, Mademoiselle. I am looking for Commander Hermion. He is needed at the headquarters," he replied.

Linette laughed, *"Then you will have to carry him."* She opened the door fully to show the unconscious man prone in the chair.

The officer made a face then shrugged.

"I see. The fool cannot take alcohol. Any more than half a bottle and he just passes out. It happens every time. Where is his bag?"

Linette pointed at the now relocked bag propped by the chair. *"It is where he dropped it."*

"Good, I will take that as it has the information that is needed. I will send a couple of men over in an hour or so to help him home," he said and bent down to pick it up.

Linette held her breath as one glance the wrong way and he would see Marty under the bed, but he just stood and tucked the bag under his arm.

She forced herself to take a slow breath.

"You should not waste your time on this fool," he said, *"However, if you are looking for companionship with someone who won't pass out on you, then it would be my pleasure to entertain you."*

"You are very gallant, Capitan," Linette smiled, thinking, *what a slimeball,* and opened the door for him to leave.

"I will bear that in mind next time I feel in need of company," she told him with a smile.

She waved a little, coy goodbye as he went through the door. She closed it, leaned back on it and let out a huge sigh of relief as Marty crawled out from under the bed, slid a stiletto back into the sheath on his forearm, and started brushing off the dust bunnies he had picked up.

"Interesting," said Marty, *"I better get out of here before they arrive. See you at breakfast."*

The next morning, he met Linette as usual and she told him that two Lieutenants had turned up and half-carried, half-dragged the commandant back to his quarters.

They left on a 'tour of inspection' of the depots and assembly areas as they had for the last few weeks. Half-way around when they were visiting a remote warehouse, Marty suddenly asked, *"What date is it?"*

"In the revolutionary or Gregorian calendar?" responded Linette.

"The one we use in England."

He had never heard of the Gregorian calendar.

"The twenty-eighth of February, 1798," laughed Linette.

"It's my birthday!" said Marty, *"I'm seventeen today."*

"Congratulations, Mon Chere," Linette said and kissed him on the cheek.

Just then, a man in a grey suit walked up to them.

"Why are you concerned with the date in England?" he asked.

Marty realised he had made a mistake. The man was obviously secret police and must have overheard what he had said. He was the last person they wanted paying attention to them.

Linette stepped forward and asked,

"who are you and what business is that of yours?"

Marty looked around. There wasn't anybody else in sight.

"Citizen Caron, security police," he replied, *"Now, would you be so kind as to answer my question."*

"We are inspectors for the ministries of war and supply," Linette explained, *"We need to keep abreast of the dates in England as our schedule is linked to what the Roast Beefs are doing."*

"I don't think so," Citizen Caron replied, "I clearly heard your friend say, 'The one we use in England.' I think you will accompany me to our headquarters for further questioning and for us to verify your identity."

That was enough for Marty. With a final scan of the surroundings, he moved out from behind Linette and his hand flashed out and back. Caron looked at him with a look of surprise and said,

"What did you just do?"

Then, he sighed and slid to the ground quite dead.

Linette looked down at him and at the tiny patch of blood on his jacket that lined up with the gap between his fourth and fifth ribs.

"Very professional," she said with the merest touch of irony. "Now, what do we do with him?"

Marty pointed over to their left with his still bloody stiletto, "He becomes lunch for those guys."

"Pigs? You want to feed him to the pigs?" Linette replied, looking slightly queasy.

Marty pulled out a small bottle of brandy. "Douse him with this and throw him in there. There was an old boy from the mines got drunk one night and fell into a pigpen on his way home. But the time they found him they had eaten half of him. By the time someone finds him, they won't be able to tell he was stabbed and just assume he got drunk and fell in."

Linette thought about it for a second or two then bent to take the feet of the rapidly cooling corpse. Together, they carried him to the pen and dropped him in. There were about twenty pigs in there that should make short work of him.

It was a hell of way to celebrate his birthday but any day they reduced the numbers of the secret police was a good day.

The next time he saw Armand, he was wearing a pink handkerchief sticking out of his breast pocket. That was a signal that they had new instructions. That evening, Marty went for a walk and when he found a particular signpost, he looked for a stone pointing due East-West. Making sure there was no one watching him, he picked up the stone and removed a folded paper from below it.

Back in his room, he decoded the message.

Happy Birthday

We need to have the date that they will set sail and if possible, the destination.

Short and to the point, he thought as he burnt both the original and the decoded copy.

There is only a couple of ways to get that, he thought and went to find Linette.

She wasn't in the Café, so he went to her room and knocked. There was a noise, but the door stayed shut. He knocked again. There was a muffled scream? He wasn't sure but tried the handle it was locked. This time, there was definitely a muffled scream! He stood back, pulled his pistols, and kicked the door just below the lock. It wasn't much of a door and less of a lock and burst inwards as the lock hasp gave way. Inside, he saw Linette on the bed with a figure standing over her holding her down with one hand over her mouth.

"You! get away from her and stand aside!" He barked. The man's head turned, and he saw it was the smarmy captain of infantry that had come to find the commandant. He was obviously drunk and had a mad look in his eyes. His trousers were undone, and he was obviously in a state of arousal. Marty levelled his right-hand pistol at the erect member and said in an even voice,

"If you want to keep that soldier boy, let – her – go."

With one pistol pointing right between his eyes and the other straight at his manhood, both the madness and his ardour faded. He looked at Marty with a bemused expression then at Linette then down at his crutch. The drunken madness faded from his eyes.

"Oh my god, what have I done," he cried in a wretched voice.

Marty pushed him over to the chair and made him sit down.

"Do your trousers up, you animal," Marty snarled.

The sound of steps could be heard coming up the stairs. Linette jumped off the bed, tucked her exposed breasts back into her dress, and quickly shut the door. There was a knock and a voice called, *"Mademoiselle, are you alright? We heard shouting."*

She opened the door a crack and said, *"Why, yes I am fine. I didn't hear anything. It must have come from outside."*

"If you are sure," said the voice that didn't sound very convinced.

"I am fine," she reassured him, *"Really, I am."*

She shut the door and leaned on it as footsteps receded down the stairs.

"Now you," she said and started towards the Capitan.

"A moment before you castrate him," Marty intervened. He led her to the far corner of the room, keeping one of his pistols on the Capitan at all times. He quickly whispered to her about the message from Armand and outlined an idea that had come to him while she was at the door.

He led them back in front of the wretched man.

"You are?" Marty asked.

"Capitan Louise Jambon," he replied.

"You know we are from the ministry?" Marty continued.

"Yes," he replied.

"Do you know of the Department of Internal Security?" Marty asked.

"Oh God," he moaned.

"What do you know?" Linette asked.

"They ensure that secrets are kept and root out the real traitors. They aren't like the secret police who are just looking for people who don't believe in the revolution."

"Exactly," said Marty and gave him a look that he hoped was meaningful. It worked; a look of horror came over his face.

"And you are both agents of . . ."

Marty and Linette nodded.

Jambon hung his head into his hands and moaned. In his mind, he could see the blade of a guillotine falling towards his neck. He had tried to rape a member of the dreaded Department and if they didn't kill him, then his wife would.

He had nowhere to go.

Marty and Linette let him ponder his fate. She sat on the bed and Marty put his guns away then leaned against the wall. He was tempted to take out a stiletto and clean his nails or something equally menacing but decided that doing nothing was probably even more terrifying.

The silence stretched out.

The Jambon looked up and said, *"What can I do to redeem myself? I am not a bad man I love my country, and I love my wife, believe it or not."*

Linette refrained from answering that and put the mission in front of her personal desire to cut his nuts off.

"You can help us," she said, *"We believe that there is a leak from the central staff, and we need to get into the headquarters without alerting the individual that we are on to him."*

Jambon looked at them with a desperate look and said, *"If I do this, can this 'incident' be forgotten?"*

Marty looked at him, "You are in no position to bargain but *I can promise it will never appear on your record or be made public,"* he said with absolute sincerity.

Jambon looked from him to Linette and back. The look *she* gave him made him cringe.

"OK, I will do what you ask," he said in a resigned tone.

"Go," Marty instructed, *"be at the café next to this hotel at eight o'clock tomorrow evening. Tell your wife you have special duties if she asks why you are out in the evening and do not wear your uniform."*

Jambon left with his head bowed and his trousers firmly fastened.

Chapter 15: A Little Bit of 'Breaking and Entering'

They met at the designated time, and Marty told Jambon,

"We need to get into the Comandante's office and inspect his papers. Can you get us in unobserved?"

Jambon looked surprised for a moment but then a look of understanding crossed his face.

"Aah, you suspect his sexual preferences have made him vulnerable," he said with a smirk.

"The reason is none of your concern," Linette snapped, *"Can you get us in?"*

A little abashed at her curt response he replied, *"There is a hatch to the cellar at the rear of the building that could be used to get in, but it is locked with a padlock and I have no key."*

"The padlock is on the outside?" asked Marty.

"Yes, it is used to deliver firewood," he explained.

They left the table and walked the short distance to the headquarters building. It was dark, and a sleepy sentry stood outside the main door. Jambon led them around the building to the rear and through a gate to a courtyard. The hatch was against the back wall and protruded a couple of inches above ground level, the padlock was sturdy but a regular pattern. Marty knelt and, by touch, picked the lock in less than fifteen seconds.

They gently lifted the hatch, hoping it didn't squeak too loudly. Once it was open, Marty located the wooden ladder that led down into the pitch-dark cellar. He very carefully climbed down feeling for every rung with his feet. Once he reached the bottom, he took a small shuttered lantern from his shoulder bag and lit the candle inside. The lantern had a polished metal reflector and was designed to throw a weak beam of light forward through the glass. He shone it on the ladder. First, Jambon came down then Linette, who carefully lowered the hatch back into place.

Marty motioned Jambon to lead the way and they made their way to the other end of the cellar where there was a stair that they climbed to find a door at the top. It was latched from the other side.

Marty gave Jambon the lantern and delved into his bag. He pulled out a strip of springy metal, which he carefully worked between the door and the jam then slid it up to lift the catch on the other side. He reached over and closed the shutter on the lantern then slowly started to move the door. He felt a slight resistance and heard the start of a squeak. He stopped, shut the door, and opened the shutter again.

He took a small stoppered bottle from his coat pocket and a hollow straw. He opened the bottle, dipped the straw in it, and put his finger over the open end. He then pulled the straw out and held it at the top of the lowest hinge. Removing his finger, he allowed a drop or two of oil to escape from the straw and lubricate the hinge. He repeated this on all three hinges.

They waited for a few minutes, during which Jambon was starting to fidget.

"What is your problem?" hissed Linette.

"I need to pee," he replied, *"I am very nervous."*

Linette stood to one side and indicated he should go back down into the cellar and relieve himself. He took the lantern with him and soon, they heard the unmistakable sound of urine hitting the dirt floor.

"The man has the bladder of an 'orse," she whispered in Marty's ear who had to restrain himself from laughing.

Jambon returned and Marty had him close the lantern again. He tried the door and this time, it opened with the only the faintest of grumbles. They stepped into a corridor, and Jambon led them up to the second floor to the Commandant's office. They left him outside on 'watch' as they didn't want him to see what they would be doing.

The room had shutters on the inside of the windows, which they closed and then opened the lantern. They searched the desktop and found nothing of interest, then unlocked and searched each drawer. Still nothing. There was a cabinet with a roller shutter against one wall which Linette opened after picking the lock. Inside, was a bank of drawers each with a label, and a quick scan showed that most were dated but one just had the word "Expedition" written on it.

Linette pulled it out completely and took the drawer to the desk. They went through it, page by page, in astonishment. The papers inside were copies of orders from Paris showing that General Napoleon himself had ordered an army of some forty thousand men be assembled in a number of ports around the Mediterranean and that they had to be ready to embark on a fleet to be assembled at Toulon by the beginning of April. The fleet at Toulon was to be made up of thirteen ships of the line, fourteen frigates, and four hundred transports and was to be supplemented by ships from Genoa, Civitavecchia and Bastia. Marty scribbled down the numbers as fast as he could while Linette looked in vain for a destination for the "Expedition."

They had been in the room for almost an hour when there was a faint scratch at the door. Marty went to see what the problem was while Linette returned the room to its untouched state. Jambon was obviously very, very nervous by now and waiting outside on his own hadn't helped. So, Marty stood with him in a deliberately relaxed manner until Linette left the room to join him. Marty stuck his head through the door and glanced around the room. He almost closed the door when he noticed that the shutters were still closed. He raised his eyebrows at Linette and went and opened them. Satisfied that they had left no trace, Marty led the way back to the cellar.

Once outside and back at the café, they thanked Jambon for his cooperation and said that would take care not to mention that he had helped them in their report. He looked mightily relieved at that and scurried away without even saying goodbye.

Chapter 16: A Sea Chase

It was now imperative to get the information back to Armand and to get out of Toulon as soon as possible. Luckily, the next day was a scheduled drop day, so they grabbed their things from their rooms and set off to Sanary to try and intercept him as he came ashore. They got there just after dawn and settled down in a spot where they were concealed but could keep an eye on the old wooden dock that jutted out to sea.

Around nine o'clock, a fishing boat approached from offshore and tied up at the dock. They didn't recognise it, but the unmistakeable figure of Armond climbed out and strolled down to the shore while the crew were busy offloading fish in baskets. He stopped to talk to a man that had emerged from a shed set back from the beach who then beckoned for the crew to carry the baskets in. As soon as they had all gone inside, Armand started walking along the path towards their hiding place. Marty and Linette stepped out onto the path and strolled over towards him.

"What the hell are you doing here?" he asked in total surprise.

"We'll tell you later, but we need to go now!" Marty told him.

They didn't bother to hide the fact that they joined the fishing boat or the fact that it left in a hurry when Armand shouted to the crew to get back on board. They didn't think they would be coming back.

Once back on the Alouette, one of the crew chopped a hole in the bottom of the fishing boat to sink before they set sail for Gibraltar.

The next morning, their luck ran out. Dawn came and with it, two sets of sails on the horizon. The lookout immediately identified them as French frigates, that turned and headed their way as soon they were spotted. They put on as much sail as they could and headed Southwest as fast as they were able as they couldn't stand up to close inspection. But by around midday, they could see that the Frigates were hull up and gaining. Their bottom was in need of a clean and in any case, even on their best day, the corvette would never outrun a Frigate who with their longer hull were more hydrodynamically efficient.

A swift calculation showed the French ships would be in range with their fore chasers about an hour before sunset at the rate they were gaining.

"We need an extra hour," Marty said and asked the master, "How much more speed do we need to stay out of range until dark?"

"Another two knots," Monk replied. He was a member of the Deal brotherhood and had been the Master of a cargo ship in his day.

"How can we make that?" asked Armand.

"The only way is to lighten her," Monk replied, "if we dump most of the water and the guns, we might just do it."

Marty looked over at his beloved carronades and sighed.

"So be it," said Armand "let's get to it"

The whole crew was put to work and each barrel was hoisted quickly from its carriage and dropped over the side to be followed by the carriage itself. A second team used axes to stove in the tops of the water barrels and empty the contents into the bilges. Then a team got on the chain pump and pumped the water overboard as fast as they could. That was such hard work that they had to change the hands on the pump every ten minutes.

They cast the log. They had gained two fathoms under two knots in speed. The French were still gaining but they had bought a bit more time.

Marty looked at the map and estimated that they were somewhere between Mercia and Algiers. He looked up and saw that Armand had the crew wetting the sails.

There was a bang from behind them. He ran to the stern rail and looked back at the frighteningly close frigates just in time to see a splash as a shot landed some ways behind and to the left of their wake. A dirty puff of smoke came from the bow of the closest one and he watched in fascination as the dark blob of another ball came towards them and dropped into the sea a cable short but in line.

He checked the pennant. It showed the wind had shifted direction slightly.

"Bring her up as close to the wind as she will sail," he ordered the man on the wheel and called to the men to brace up the sheets.

Armand stepped over, and Marty pointed out that with their rig they could sail a little closer to the wind than the Frigates and that would give them a tiny advantage.

Sure enough, they could see that the French were having trouble maintain their course and were falling off half a point. They might just make it as now the gap was staying the same as the courses diverged a little.

More bangs and a ball splashed down level with them.

"The buggers are overcharging their guns to get our range!" said Tom, who had moved up near to where Marty was stood.

They looked across to the Western horizon and could see that the sun was just kissing it. Another twenty minutes and they would be safe in the dark. But could they avoid getting hit until then?

"Oh shit!" exclaimed Tom, and Marty wrenched his attention back to the frigates. The divergent course had allowed the Frenchman to present his broadside to them and the side of the ship now blossomed with a row of flashes and puffs of smoke. Splashes of skipping shot raced across the sea towards them. Marty's eyes went wide, and he heard Linette scream from behind him. One shot was dead in line and bounced once, then twice, and then a third time before thudding into their side.

The Alouette shuddered at the impact of the twelve-pound ball, smacking into her just above the waterline with the heel they had on. Marty went below to check on the damage. The ball had lost most of its momentum as it skipped but it still had enough energy to spring the plank and Marty got a team together to shore up the damaged area as best, they could. By the time he got back on deck, it was dark, Armand had extinguished all lights, and was about to change course to throw off their pursuers.

"Will it hold?" he asked.

"Should do, as long as the seas don't get any rougher," Marty replied.

"Silence in the ship! Prepare to wear!" Armand ordered, "Steer due South," he told the helmsman, "Wear ship!"

They continued South for two hours and then swung back West towards Gibraltar. The lookouts reported nothing until dawn when they heard

"SAIL HO! Three points off the Starboard Aft Quarter!"

Marty raced up the ratlines of the mainmast and looked along the horizon.

Dammit it's them Frenchie's again, he thought as he spotted their topsails.

He waved at Armand and shouted out what he could see and then got down on deck as fast as he could.

"Their captain must have a sixth sense," he said in exasperation to Armand, as they went to the charts.

"All we can do is stay as close to the wind as possible, try and head a point South of West and pray we get to Gibraltar or meet a British ship before they catch us," Armand concluded after studying the North African coastline closely on the chart. "There isn't anywhere to hide."

"We better pray the wind doesn't shift in their favour as well," Marty gloomily replied.

The chase continued. The men didn't have much to do except trim the sails and watch the two French ships get slowly closer and idle hands tend to get nervous. Marty started weapons practice to give them something to do and to make it more interesting, he matched up men from different watches. It soon turned into a good-natured contest and covered blade work, pistol shooting, and unarmed combat.

That took them up to lunch time when the men broke off the contests to eat their midday meal. Marty, Armand, and Linette ate together in the captain's cabin. They were largely silent as they ate as they could see the French frigates through the transom windows, and they were an oppressive presence.

Marty felt something in the way the ship was moving. He left the table and went out onto the deck. He checked the pennant and saw that the wind had swung a little more West. He looked to the horizon and saw a bank of dark cloud, approaching from the South-Southwest.

An hour later, the cloudbank had developed into a heaving mass with lightning playing along the forward edge. The wind was increasing rapidly and moaning through the rigging. Armand and Marty were getting worried about the masts as well as the damaged hull, but the frigates showed no sign of taking in sail, so they had no option but to keep as much on as possible as well. Marty had extra lookouts posted to keep watch for squalls and had the men ready to reduce sail at a moment's notice.

The weather went from getting bad to very bad rapidly and they had no choice but to take in the mains and reef the tops. Armand looked back at the frigates.

"Those idiots are still keeping on full sail," he shouted over the now howling wind.

Marty turned and looked just as one of the lookouts yelled,

"SQUALL!!"

They saw the wind devil as the squall came across the water. It flattened the tops of the waves and looked as if it was arrowing straight at them from just off the larboard bow.

"Hard to Starboard!" Marty ordered and threw himself on to the wheel to help the helmsmen.

The ship complained as she turned and the wind came more from the beam, but she responded, and they hung on as the edge of the squall brushed against their stern. The ship felt as if it had been kicked and started to turn back to larboard as the wind pushed on the stern quarter.

The squall passed and they watched as it rushed down on the Frigates that had caught up to about three cables astern of them. It slammed into the leading one, her foresails were shredded with a ripping boom and the foremast snapped about two thirds of the way up. The ship slewed and they saw that the mainsail had also torn loose and was flapping in the wind. The second Frigate took evasive action as the leading one slowed and turned towards it, steering hard to starboard, causing her sails to go into confusion as they spilled the wind and she went into irons.

Before anyone on the Alouette could comment or even think, another squall hit them on the beam and the ship healed so far over that they were convinced they would capsize. Everything that wasn't tied down went over the side, including a couple of men. The Alouette struggled to right herself and in the end, she won as she slowly came back onto an almost even keel.

A quick look aloft showed that the masts were bare of sails, they were fighting for survival now. Armand quickly ordered a storm sail set on the fore and steered to run before the storm to keep the sea on their stern.

He sent Marty below to check on their jury-rigged repairs. It wasn't good but it could have been worse. They were leaking but the planks were holding – for now they could keep ahead of it with the pumps. When Marty got back on deck, he couldn't see the French anywhere.

They pumped the ship every four hours for two days before the storm left them. The crew was exhausted and hungry as they had no rest and nothing but cold rations. Linette had been confined to her cabin as she was so sea-sick, she could barely move.

They turned back to the West and headed to Gibraltar with a sense of relief.

Chapter 17: The Hunt Is On

They reached Gibraltar by the end of March only to be told the Fleet was at the Tagus. So, they stocked up with food and water and set off to find them. They finally got there by the sixth of April, showed their number and dispatches, which got a 'Captain report aboard" signal in return from the Flagship.

Armand, Marty, and Linette all went across climbed up onto the deck of the Flagship to be greeted by a surprised first lieutenant. He couldn't keep his eyes off Linette, who was wearing trousers and a shirt, that didn't hide the fact she was a woman.

Armand gave him the letter written by Admiral Hood and asked to see the admiral. The lieutenant scoffed at first, then read the letter, looked the three of them over again, and went to the captain. The captain looked quizzically at the three of them as the lieutenant spoke to him on the quarterdeck and read the letter himself. His eyebrows shot up, and he sent a midshipman to the admiral with the letter and a message. Five minutes later, a flag lieutenant appeared, introduced himself as Frederick Fitzwilliam, and escorted them to the admiral's quarters.

They entered after being announced by the customary bellow of the Marine guard. Admiral St. Vincent was sitting behind a desk talking to another Admiral who was a small man with one arm and a scar across one of his eyes.

The small man stood and addressed them in a somewhat high pitched nasally voice with a Norfolk accent.

"I am Rear Admiral Nelson. Your letter says that you are working on special duties for Admiral Hood but it doesn't say who you are or what those duties are. Please introduce yourselves and explain."

Armand introduced himself using his best English accent. "Armand Clavell Lieutenant Royal Navy. Formally, Lieutenant of the Royal French Navy at your service."

Then he introduced Marty and Linette.

"Midshipman Martin Stockley and Linette." Nelson raised his eyebrows at the omission of her surname, but Armand continued. "Midshipman Stockley and Linette have been gathering intelligence in Toulon concerning the build-up of troops and ships in the Mediterranean."

Nelson looked at the two of them and was about to say something when Admiral St. Vincent said,

"Horatio, why don't we just see what they have to report and then you can ask questions."

Nelson nodded and sat down. Armand gestured for Marty to carry on.

"Sir, we have discovered that General Bonaparte has assembled a force of greater than four hundred transports, thirteen ships of the line with fourteen frigates, and more than thirty-five thousand troops. They are to be ready to sail by the end of April and will be reinforced by more ships from Genoa. We have been unable to discover the destination for this Expeditionary Force as it is called by the French military. Apparently, there are only two or three people who know that. Napoleon being one of them."

"And how did you discover this?" asked St. Vincent.

"Linette and I broke into the Military Headquarters in Toulon and read the orders from Bonaparte to his commanders," answered Marty.

Both the Admirals eyebrows shot up in amazement at that and at the level delivery without a hint of boasting.

"Miss Linette," said Nelson, "are we to believe that you and this young midshipman walked into Toulon, infiltrated the headquarters of the French Military, and stole secrets that must have been heavily guarded?" his tone spoke of his disbelief.

"Oui Admiral, that is correct. Martin speaks French like a native and we posed as operatives of the ministries of war and supply. Then we found someone we could persuade we were really from the Department of Internal Security investigating a suspected spy in the headquarters staff. He let us in to the building and we were able to search the office of the commandant and find the papers."

"Sounds like a story from the penny dreadfuls," snorted Nelson.

"Sir," said Armand, "Our ship and crew are part of the Special Operations Flotilla set up by Admiral Hood and Mr. Wickham and are trained to infiltrate the enemy and gather intelligence."

"Aah Wickham," said St. Vincent, "I thought I could smell his hands on this. I heard he and Hood were up to something. Well, do you have a written report of your findings?"

"Yes sir," said Marty and handed over a sealed report.

St. Vincent opened it, then called for his flag lieutenant.

"Please take these officers and young lady into my coach cabin and get them some food. I want a report on the state of their ship, any repairs it needs and what happened to their guns," he ordered.

Once they were in the coach cabin, Marty said to the Fitzwilliam. "He doesn't miss much, does he?"

"He doesn't miss anything," Fitzwilliam replied.

"Now about your ship. French built corvette, isn't she?"

"Yes we, aah, borrowed her from the French," replied Marty.

"Cut her out?" Fitzwilliam asked.

"In a manner of speaking," Marty laughed, "she is very useful as with French flag the average French Captain just accepts her for what she appears to be."

"The guns?" Fitzwilliam prompted.

"Had to dump them overboard," Marty replied, "We were being chased by a pair of French Frigates and needed to run for it. They were French nine pounders and a few carronades."

"Damage?"

"Sprung plank below the waterline on the larboard side from a French ball, a bottom that needs cleaning and rigging that could do with tensioning. The storm that saved us from the frigates gave us a beating for two days."

"Frigates?" Fitzwilliam said and then held up his hand to stop Marty from answering that.

"I'm sure the details are in the report and the admiral will tell me if needed. Now, eat and I will arrange for your ship to be hauled out and repaired on the careenage. I will also see if we can round up a few nine pounders to replace the ones you lost. I believe we had another ex-French sloop here that had her mainmast ripped out in a storm. Her guns are ashore as her hull was condemned."

They ate the food the steward brought them and fine fare it was! Roast beef and chicken with fresh vegetables and bread. They drank diluted lime juice rather than wine and were drinking a cup of tea when they were asked to attend the admirals again.

This time, there were three chairs set in front of the desk, and St. Vincent indicated they were to sit.

"Your report is extraordinary," he opened "if it is all true," he held his hand up at the looks of concern on their faces, "and I believe it is, you have performed a valuable service. Nelson and I have discussed what should be done, and we agree that we must send an expedition of our own to Toulon to try and intercept this armada. We, in fact, received orders from the admiralty three days ago to prepare for this as Lord Spencer is concerned by information they have already received."

"Yes," said Nelson, "I will lead a force of three liners and three frigates plus a Sloop."

He gave them a significant look.

"Yes, you will be coming with us. We will leave at the end of the month, so make sure your ship is ready."

St. Vincent added, "I will write to Hood and inform him of the successful completion of your mission and that we are borrowing you for a while. Miss Linette, if you want to go back to England, you can take passage on the packet."

"Thank you, Admiral," she replied, "I will."

"You two gentlemen and your very French ship are required to attend Admiral Nelson for 'special duties'," He smiled.

Lieutenant Fitzwilliam was as good as his word. They were warped over to the careenage and a team of carpenters from ships around the fleet descended on the Alouette. In a little over seven days, the offending planking had been replaced and her bottom cleaned. She was re-floated and her rigging replaced where it was damaged beyond repair, and re-tensioned. She was warped to the dock and had new cannon lifted onboard. They had to offload all their French shot as it wasn't the same calibre as the British and bring aboard the correct British ammunition. Their powder had been off loaded with all their stores while they were careened and that all had to be reloaded and stored, but with the help of what had to be a double crew of men from other ships, it was done in record time.

Nelson sailed his flagship, the Vanguard, a seventy-four-gun, third rate to Gibraltar, collected his squadron, The Orion, Alexander, Emerald, Terpsichore and Bonne Citoyenne, and sailed into the Mediterranean on the ninth of May. The Alouette followed along like a puppy. It all went wrong on the eleventh when they ran straight into the teeth of a massive storm in the Gulf of Lion. The Vanguard was seriously damaged and had to be towed by the Alexander to Sardinia where she carried out repairs.

Once completed, they set off for Toulon, arriving on the thirty-first of May. Nelson ordered the Alouette to take a look into the harbour. It was completely empty.

Armand ordered the helmsman to steer for the nearest guard boat and heave to within hailing distance.

"Where has everyone gone?" he asked.

The boat steered over until it was alongside and hooked onto the chains.

"I was ordered to sail here and join a fleet!" he added with a very gallic wave of the arms that took in the entire anchorage.

"You are too late, Captain," replied the sergeant of Marine in the boat.

"Too late?" cried Armand, *"Too late? Mon dieu. My orders are to deliver dispatches to Admiral Brueys d'Aigalliers. We were delayed because we had to make repairs after a big storm in the Gulf of Lion."*

"Well, they left ten or eleven days ago and the word was that they headed South towards Sicily," the Sergeant told him.

"Thank you, my friend," Armand told him and tossed him a bottle of brandy. He bellowed orders to get them underway again.

Four hours later, he was in the admiral's cabin on the Vanguard in front of Nelson and his flag captain.

"So, we believe from what the guard boat told us that the fleet left around the nineteenth and headed South towards Sicily," he concluded.

"And you posed as a French ship, so they had no reason to lie?" asked Nelson.

"Yes, we gave them no reason to believe we were anything else. We have a full set of uniforms for such an occasion, so I believe the information is accurate," replied Armand.

"Well, we can't leave here until the rest of my fleet arrives," Nelson stated, obviously frustrated, "and all the time we wait, the further ahead they get."

And wait they did until on the seventh of June, Thomas Troubridge arrived with ten ships of the line and a fourth rate. Nelson ordered the Alouette to stay with them as a messenger. They sailed to Elba and then on to Naples where it was reported by the Ambassador that the French had been seen passing in the direction of Malta.

Onboard the Alouette, the Deal boys were beginning to complain at the amount of time they had been away from home without any potential profit. Armand and Marty were treading a fine line; whilst they were Navy officers, the majority of their crew were privateers, and that was something they hadn't dared share with Nelson.

Marty bought them some time by pointing out that if there was a major engagement with the French fleet, they would stand to take a share in the prizes if they were in sight of the action. He also promised them that once they were released by Nelson, they would take as many prizes as they could on their way home.

The Alouette was acting as an advanced picket, ranging ahead of the fleet when they came upon a Brig sailing from Ragusa on the twenty second of June. They were told that the French had sailed from Malta Eastwards on the sixteenth of June. Nelson and his captains deduced from that, Napoleon was en-route to Alexandria, and they changed course to make their way directly there.

They arrived on the twenty eighth of June and there was no sign of the French. After talking with a highly sceptical city commander, Nelson ordered the fleet to sail North to Syracuse where he would re-provision. While they were in port, he wrote many letters and dispatches and, much to Armand and Marty's disappointment, ordered the Alouette to return to England with them.

Chapter 18: Make The Most..

So, they set sail with no prizes and no big fleet action to line their pockets. Marty and Armand had a problem.

Then Marty had an inspiration.

"The French have taken Malta, right?" he asked Armand.

"Mai oui. It is now under their control," Armand replied.

"And the garrison there will need to be supplied and the easiest way for that to be done is to send supplies from Toulon or Marseille?" Marty continued.

"Oui."

"Then we can probably count on a couple of fat merchantmen running back and forth then."

"Certainment," grinned Armand.

"Time for some piracy?"

"Absolument!" laughed Armand.

They got out the charts and figured that the French merchantmen would have to pass between the Island of Pantellaria and Sicily to get to Malta. So, if they took a course that steered them up the most likely route from Malta through the gap and on to a point South of Sardinia, they would have the best chance of finding a target.

The weather was fine with a steady North Westerly breeze and that meant they had to tack back and forth to make headway, which luckily, meant they covered more potential routes of any ships sailing in the opposite direction.

After two days, they spotted a sail and changed course to intercept. It was a French Merchantman. She was heading Southeast and heavily laden as she was low in the water. It didn't take them long to catch up to her and they approached with a French flag streaming from their stern. As soon as they got within two cables, they showed their true colours and ran out the guns. To their astonishment, their prey ran out hers as well and fired off a broadside of four six-pounders.

"Zut Allors!" said Armand.

Marty laughed and ordered a broadside of chain shot to be fired into their rigging.

The guns barked, and smoke billowed. When it cleared, they saw the merchantman wallowing under backed sails and the flag coming down. Their rigging was cut in several places and their mainsail was shredded.

A boarding crew led by Marty soon had the ship under control, and they identified her as a French built Brig/Sloop out of Marseilles called the Ellen Louise. She was carrying leather, wine, brandy, hams, sausage, fine cloth and the personal belongings of several senior officers of the occupying French forces that was following them to Malta.

"It's a keeper," Marty called across.

"Ok, you command her," Armand called back, "I will send you another ten men."

Marty ended up with a crew of fifteen, including the shadow six who as usual managed to stay close to him.

They resumed their course Northwest albeit a bit slower as they could only travel as fast as the prize. All the same they picked up two more prizes and had a healthy little convoy. Then the weather suddenly turned. A fierce Mediterranean storm swept in from the North and stuck with them for three days. It was as much as they could do to stay afloat, their mainmast was snapped off half way up and they got separated from the other ships.

When the weather cleared, they did their best to jury rig a top half to the main mast and got her underway again, but all they could achieve was about four knots. Marty hoped they could make Gibraltar where they could affect better repairs, but it was going to be slow going.

"Sail Ho!" called down the lookout, "Looks like the Alouette from her topsails."

That would be a miracle, thought Marty as he grabbed a telescope and shinnied up the ratlines to try and see for himself. *It could be*, he thought as the similarity was striking. One thing he could be sure of the ship was heading their way.

It only took an hour or so for the ship to get close enough that they could clearly see her hull and that it wasn't the Alouette. It could be her twin, but the differences were obvious to Marty. As she came closer still, Marty prepared his men to try and bluff it out and convince the Corvette's Captain they were French.

They hove to when commanded and waited while a boat came over. Marty was surprised when the captain himself climbed up the tumble home and appeared over the side followed closely by a dozen heavily armed sailors. He looked at Marty and the crew then turned and waved to his ship. All the gun ports opened, and they ran out their guns.

"I don't know who you are but you are not the crew of this ship. Where is my brother, the captain?" he asked in French and drew his sword.

Marty knew they could overpower the boarding party but faced with the guns of the Corvette, he knew they wouldn't stand a chance afterwards. So, he replied in English,

"I am sorry. I don't speak French. Martin Stockley, Midshipman Royal Navy at your service," and he sketched a bow. "Tom, please bring the French skipper here," He added.

The Corvette captain didn't say anything, just waited, and when the Ellen Louise's captain came up from below, he smiled and said, *"Anton! Are you well? Did they treat you properly?"*

"Yes, I am alright Stephan," Anton replied, *"The Roast Beef treated me well enough. Beware this young cockerel speaks perfect French as do half his crew."*

"Really?" Stephan replied and looked at Marty with renewed interest.

"Now, what would the British need a French speaking crew for? Well, we will find out in good time."

He then addressed Marty directly, *"You and your men will be transferred to my ship. Do you give your parole?"*

Marty knew the game was up for now and replied, *"No, sir. I will not abandon my men."*

"Very gallant of you. Please place all your weapons on the deck in front of you, and you will be searched, so don't play games," Captain Stephan replied.

"Drop your weapons," he ordered, "All of them"

They were grouped together on the foredeck and taken in two groups across to the Corvette.

She is identical to the Alouette, Marty thought.

He was separated from his men and taken to the captain's cabin. The guard stood him in front of the desk and made him stand while they waited for the captain to return. He felt the ship get under way and turn so the wind was almost on her stern.

Malta then, he thought.

The captain returned and sat at his desk. He looked at Marty for a long moment.

"How old are you?"

"Seventeen."

"How long have you been a midshipman?"

"Four years."

"Where did you learn to speak French?"

"Onboard ship. The Navy run French classes to improve the men's minds."

"Don't try and be clever with me. I will have you whipped. How many of your men speak French?"

"Only a few, maybe four or five."

"What are you doing in the Mediterranean?"

No answer.

The captain nodded to the guard, who stepped around and punched Marty in the stomach, folding him up so he landed on his hands and knees on the deck planking. The blow had caught him right under the diaphragm and knocked every bit of air out of him. He was retching and trying to breath at the same time. The guard grabbed Marty by the collar and dragged him to his feet.

"I repeat. What were you doing in the Mediterranean?"

"Fuck off."

The guard hit him again and this time, he followed it up with a couple of solid kicks to his ribs then dragged his head up by his hair and punched him in the mouth. He dragged him to his feet again.

"Same question."

"We were here with the Fleet. We were sent home with dispatches and grabbed a couple of prizes on the way."

"Where is the fleet now?"

"No idea. We left them in Sicily."

The captain looked at him for a long moment.

"I think you know more than you are saying, but the authorities in Malta will loosen your tongue. Take him to the bread room and lock him in there."

Chapter 19: Escape

Marty was half-dragged, half-led down to the bread room and thrown inside into the pitch dark. He stayed still for a while, checking his breathing and running his hands over his body. Two or even three broken ribs he guessed. He wasn't coughing up blood, so that was manageable. He was bleeding from a split lip and it felt like he had a loose tooth, but he was still operational. That was all that counted.

That fucker is going to pay for that, he thought then reached down and took off his boots.

He had made sure he was wearing his lace up calf boots when they realised they would be boarded. He started picking at the stitching of the seam that ran around the top of the upper of his right boot. It came away easily and he worked his fingers in between the layers.

A moment later, he pulled out the blade of a cutthroat razor which he tied to his forearm with a scrap of cloth he tore from the hem of his shirt. He then removed the laces of both boots. He tied them together with an intricate Turk's head knot by touch (he had practiced tying knots with his eyes shut for hours) in the middle leaving him with around two feet of cord with a large knot in the middle.

He silently moved to the door and checked it by feel. It was exactly the same as the Alouette with a mortice lock rather than an external hasp and padlock. He went back to his boots, this time picked at the stitching on the left one producing a pair of lockpicks. He waited until he figured it was past midnight and then listened at the door again. He thought he could hear snoring. It was time to take a risk.

The lock succumbed, and he gently pushed the door to open it. It opened about a foot then stopped.

He waited. When nothing happened, he pushed his head through the gap and looked around. The space outside the door was illuminated dimly by a glim. By its light, he could see the guard was fast asleep, propped against the bulkhead with his legs across the door. He eased himself through the gap, being careful of his ribs and silenced the guard permanently by slitting his throat with the razor. He took his knife and pistol.

He slipped up the stairs on his bare feet. There was someone at the top.

He paused, listening. There weren't any voices, only the sound of the ship under reduced sail. He knew there would be at least one man on the helm.

He backed down the stairs into the shadows and scratched his knife on one of the steps. The figure at the top didn't react, so he did it again a little louder. This time, he looked around and down into the well. Marty scratched again, and the junior officer stepped down the steps. Marty stayed hidden in the shadows until he reached the bottom.

As he passed him, he quickly looped the garrotte, he had created from his bootlaces, around the sailor's throat from behind and pulled it hard at the same time as putting his knee in the small of his back. The knot crushed the man's windpipe immediately and as the shock hit, his knees buckled. Marty let him slide down until his knee was just below the nape of his neck and gave an extra hard tug. The knot was now under the doomed man's chin and the tug against the knee efficiently broke his neck. It had taken less than ten seconds to finish him off without making a sound.

He took the officer's jacket, put it on, and went up the stairs. As he came on deck, he could see the helmsman silhouetted against the starry sky and walked over as if he belonged there. He made as if he was going to look over the stern rail, but as he passed the helmsman, he clubbed him on the head with the pistol. As the sailor collapsed, he caught him under the arms and lowered him gently to the deck.

The wheel was starting to swing, so he grabbed it and used ropes to secure it in a fixed position. A quick tour of the deck found two lookouts sleeping on duty who were quickly dispatched. He couldn't believe his luck just four men on watch! This captain was an overconfident fool!

He knew the rest of his men were secured in the cable tier, so that was his next destination.

He crept through the gun deck past snoring and farting sailors in their hammocks. The smell was even more rank than on his ship and the deck was filthy, making him wish he still had his boots on. He made it to the end and slipped through the hatch into the passage to the cable tier. There was a guard who was awake and asked who was there. Marty mumbled something in French as he approached. The guard hesitated, which was a mistake, Marty stepped up close his hand clamped over the guard's mouth and his knife flashed forward under the man's ribs into his heart.

The door was padlocked but a quick search got him the keys and he opened the door to see Tom stood ready to attack whoever opened it. He relaxed as he saw it was Marty and broke out a grin in welcome.

"Get the men out and up on deck then meet me in the captain's cabin so I can give you the keys to the weapons locker and magazine," he whispered, "Try not to wake the crew on your way up."

The guard at the captain's door gave up without a fight when he found himself looking down the barrel of a pistol. He was tied up and gagged just to be sure he didn't cause any problems.

Marty crept into the cabin and up to the snoring man laid out on the cot. He smelt of wine and brandy. He thought for a second then muttered, "Sod it," and clubbed him on the head with the pistol butt. The door opened a minute later while he was hogtying the captain and Tom came in.

"A bit extreme, sir?" he said, looking at the trussed-up man.

"That fucker is responsible for doing at least two of my ribs and I might lose a tooth," snapped Marty.

"Getting all he deserved then," grinned Tom.

Marty went through the desk and found some keys, which he handed over.

"I want all our men armed with at least two pistols and a blade," he ordered.

"Put the rest of the arms under lock and key and set a guard. Then get two swivels loaded with cannister and set them up either side of the quarterdeck."

"Aye Aye, Sir," said Tom.

"Stack any bodies on deck by the mainmast. Make them look scary," he added as an afterthought.

Tom just nodded and left.

As dawn broke, they had control of the deck. They called the men up from below to start their watch, who were surprised when they found themselves looking down the wrong end of a couple of swivels manned by grinning Basques. They were also greeted with the site of the corpses of their dead comrades laid out to show off their wounds to their best advantage. Their Captain was in irons on the quarterdeck with a gun to his head. The English gave them no time to gather their wits and herded them with shouts and kicks into a group covered by the swivels.

A couple of officers and mates tried to resist but they were killed without mercy and that lesson wasn't lost on the rest of the crew as the bodies were tossed on top of the ones already on deck. Antton went amongst them, relieved them of their knives which he tossed over the side.

Brutal, uncompromising tactics and shock and awe enabled fifteen men to take over a ship manned with almost a hundred.

Marty had the captain dragged onto the main deck where a noose was rigged from the end of the mainsail yard and had him stood beneath it. He signalled the merchantman to come alongside.

The captain of the merchantman could clearly see his brother stood below the noose. Marty called across and told him that he was to do exactly what he was told, or his brother would hang. To make his point, he had Tom place the noose around his brother's neck.

When both ships were stopped about half a cable apart, Marty ordered them to send over a boat with all his and his crew's personal belongings. He sent them back with as many of the crew as they could carry.

Before they came back for the next group, he made them load the boat with brandy, wine and hams for the return trip. In this way, they took the most valuable cargo from the Merchantman and relieved themselves of the trouble of guarding a crew that outnumbered them almost seven to one.

Marty kept the captain until the last load and before he let him go, he stood in front of him and said,

"I should repay you for the beating you treated me to, but I think having to answer to your superiors why you are coming home on your brothers ship, while yours is now mine, will be revenge enough for me. But be sure though, if our paths cross again, I will gut you like the pig you are."

He then signalled to his men, and they threw the wretched man into the boat. It was halfway to the other ship when Marty had them underway and heading straight to Gibraltar.

Did he have a conscience about the dead men and the fact he had put almost a hundred men on a ship designed for thirty? Not at all, and even if he had, a pang of pain from his ribs reminded him of his treatment and he felt completely justified.

His fifteen men had to work extra hard to sail the Corvette and their progress was slow, but the weather held, and they made it to Gibraltar without too much trouble.

There, they found the Alouette with the other two prizes and they moored alongside. When Armand and the rest of the crew realised who they were, there was a great deal of good-natured insult and banter thrown back and forth.

Chapter 20: Homecoming

Marty reported to Armand, who listened without surprise to his protégé's story. He gave him twenty extra men, which would leave the Alouette short-handed, but the profit would be worth it.

Armand used Admiral Hood's letter to avoid having their prizes taken by the port admiral, and they left as soon as they could. It took two and a half weeks to make their home port, and Armand left immediately for London with the dispatches and to report to Hood and Wickham.

Blaez, his Dutch Shepherd pup, was at the farm and greeted him enthusiastically with much jumping up and licking. He had grown to be a fairly big dog in the months he had been away and could put his paws on Marty's chest if he stood on his back legs. Marty was surprised he remembered him. They spent a while getting to know each other again, and Marty resolved that he wouldn't leave him behind again.

He had Will Barbour bind his ribs to make them more comfortable and spent the first day back organising the inventory of the prize cargos and the new sloop, which was called the Hirondelle. Blaez followed him around everywhere.

The second day, he was persuaded by Bill Clarence that they could manage without him and he should rest. He returned to his office and settled down to catch up on his letter writing. He wrote to his mother, Miss Kate, Captain Turner, and the Count de Marchets. When they were finished, he got Will to take them to the local post.

He started to write to Caroline, he wasn't sure she would still want to see him after he had been away for so long, so he couched the letter in terms that left it open for her to turn him down if she wanted. He was, in fact, working himself up into quite an emotional state and was full of doubt and fear about their relationship. He was confused about his feelings for her as all this relationship malarkey was new to him and no one was around to give him any advice.

In the end, he stopped writing and decided to put the letter aside until the morning as it was getting late. Blaez, sensing his confusion sat with his head on his lap to comfort him.

He slept well and got up late. After eating, he asked Will to prepare him a bath, they had one of the new hip baths and he lowered himself into the hot water with a sigh. He still had a big, yellow and purple bruise over his ribs, but he could feel that they were slowly healing. His tooth had firmed up on its own and hadn't fallen out as he feared it would.

He was very comfortable and dozed off. He woke with the water noticeably cooler and a feeling that there was someone in the room with him. He looked around slowly and saw a figure sitting in a chair against the wall. Blaez was laying on the floor between them, just watching.

"How long have you been there," he asked.

"About half an hour," Caroline answered, "that's a nasty bruise."

"Yes. A Frenchman decided he would try and beat some secrets out of me. He broke a couple of ribs in the process," he replied with a smile.

"Did you kill him?" she asked.

"No. I took his ship instead, that's worse."

"And left an enemy behind you." It was a statement not a question.

He didn't answer that but started to stand to get out of the bath. She came to him and gave him her arm to steady himself. She also gave him a long, slow look from top to bottom with a noticeable pause in the middle.

"Do I pass inspection?" he asked.

"All looks to be present and correct, but I think we will need to check that everything is still working," she smirked.

"No time like the present," he said then paused, "Can you dry my back? I can't quite reach . . ."

Blaez decided at that point that the kitchen would be a better place to be.

The rest of the day was spent in bed, but he didn't get a huge amount of rest. That evening, he left Caroline sleeping and slipped over to the desk. He took the letter and put it on the fire.

"What was that?" she murmured.

"Just some papers," he replied and smiling happily, got back into bed.

Armand returned the next afternoon. He asked Marty to attend him in the common room. When he got there, he found most of the crew there as well.

"Gentlemen," Armand said in his quarterdeck voice, "your attention please."

The room quieted, and Marty noticed Bill Clarence stood at the back.

"I have just returned from a meeting with Admiral Hood and Mr. Wickham in London. The big news is that Nelson has destroyed the fleet that left from Toulon at the battle of Aboukir Bay. The French flag ship, the L'Orient, exploded, killing almost everyone on board. The news is in the Gazette, and I brought copies with me."

"I now have some announcements to make." He looked around the room and saw that he had their attention.

"First, the Hirondelle will be bought in by the admiral; the prize money to be distributed in the usual portions."

That got big smiles as they thought about the prize money, which would probably be a portion of forty thousand pounds.

"Second, the other two prizes and their cargos will be sold privately and Bill," he nodded to him at the back, "estimates we will get around ten thousand pounds in total for those." That raised a cheer.

"Now to other matters," he paused dramatically, "Tom Savage is now rated as coxswain and John Smith, quartermaster, they will go onto the Lark." That raised a cheer and some good-natured catcalls.

"Pete Simmons will be cox in the Alouette and Fred Bailey, the quartermaster." More cheers, he called them to order.

"As a ship has to have a captain and a Navy cutter rates a lieutenant," he paused again, glanced at Marty and then down at the ground. The men caught that, and a growl went around the room. Armand let it grow then looked up and with a grin said, "So Martin Stockley, Midshipman, will attend the Lieutenants Examination Board in Chatham next week and if 'e passes, will be immediately appointed master and commander of the Lark." The room erupted into cheering and Marty had men slapping him gently on the back, in consideration of his ribs, and shaking his hand.

Armand waited until they settled down then continued. "We will be receiving twenty new men as replacements and to increase our compliment, the usual sweepings from the gaols and magistrate's courts," he grinned at the men. "You can make sure they understand the way things are here and toe the line. We will also be getting two new mids, who have shown 'special abilities' according to our lords and masters. That is all. You are dismissed."

The room slowly emptied, and Armand led Marty back to their office where Caroline was waiting. The look on her face told him she had listened in to the whole thing, and she hugged him and gave him kiss.

"Are you ready for the exam?" she asked.

"I need to review some things but yes, I think I am," he replied.

The 'some things' kept him occupied during the daylight hours, poring over books as he discovered that he had forgotten more than he thought. Caroline left him to it and went back to her London home so as not to be a distraction. Blaez sat at his feet the whole time. Armand tutored him and threw typical scenarios at him that he knew the captains on the board liked to surprise candidates with.

Monday the seventeenth of September saw Marty in Chatham along with a dozen or so other mids in the coach of HMS Neptune awaiting their interviews with the examining board. Some mids were still poring over books trying to cram until the last minute. Others looked terrified and were visibly sweating. Some looked confident. Of those that went in; some came out crestfallen, having obviously failed and others beaming, having passed.

Marty sat quietly, just trying to stay calm and focused as his turn approached. The young man next to him went in full of confidence and came out thirty minutes later visibly shaken.

"My God, they are relentless," he stammered.

Then Marty's name was called.

He stood and straightened his uniform, lodged his hat under his arm, and entered the captain's cabin. The five captains of the Board sat behind what would have been the dining table. It had been turned into an oversized desk and they sat with their backs to the transom windows, which tended to silhouette them against the late afternoon sun.

He heard the door close behind him as he stepped up to stand beside the chair that was placed front and centre of the table.

"Midshipman Martin Stockley reporting for examination, sir." He said to the captain in the middle, who he assumed was in charge and to whom he passed his logbook and papers. He kept his eyes forward and was introduced to Captains Pellew, Franklin, Lombard, and Stonebridge. The fifth one, who he had addressed formally, was Captain Cockburn.

What followed was an intense barrage of questions from each of the board on ship handling, navigation, tactics, and even the articles of war. Then Pellew, who had been watching him carefully, suddenly asked him what he would do if he was captain of a sloop accompanying a squadron of frigates which was engaged with a stronger force of French frigates and one of the British frigates found itself broadside to broadside with a ship that outgunned it.

Marty asked where his sloop was positioned, what was the sea state, and direction and force of the wind.

Pellew gave him the information and Marty immediately visualized the scenario in his mind, working out the vectors and possibilities. Franklin was just opening his mouth to hurry him when Marty started to recite the orders he would give.

Clew up his square sails so he could wear around and make use of the prevailing wind using his fore and aft sails to speed the turn.

Swing across the Frenchman's stern and serve him with a broadside "up the arse."

He told how he would double shot his nine pounders and load his carronades with ball over cannister to do maximum damage.

He continued his narrative to describe an audacious swing across the wind to bring them back across her stern a second time.

Captain Lombard scoffed and said,

"Have you ever commanded a sloop? Those manoeuvres would see you in irons."

"Yes sir. I have had the privilege to command one as a prize and one as temporary commander. Both are written up fully in my log."

"And did you try this manoeuvre in anger?" asked Pellew.

"Yes sir. In defence of the Falcon when she was set upon by a French thirty-four. We had gotten separated by a storm, she was undermanned as we were on our way home with three prizes including the Sloop and a Frigate, but she was keeping the weather gauge and holding the Frenchman off. We came in late in the fight and raked his stern after which he blew up."

"I believe I recall reading about that action in the Gazette," put in Cockburn. "You were the mid in charge and did it with just a prize crew. Capital. Capital!"

Marty just sat and tried to look modest as he answered more questions from the rest of the board.

"Gentlemen, it's time for our verdict. Pellew, your vote?"

"He is young, but he has amassed more leadership experience than any of the others we have seen, so I say yes."

"Franklin?"

Captain Franklin was thumbing his way through Marty's log book and his eyebrows rose in surprise at some of the entries.

"Franklin?" Cockburn repeated.

"Damn boy has made more prizemoney than I have," he spluttered to the amusement of the other Captains. "I need to get a cruise. Yes, passed." (Franklin had spent most of his time in command attached to the channel fleet so had very little opportunity to take prizes.)

And so, it went down the table, Cockburn looked him in the eye and invited him to stand. Marty stood to attention.

"I am pleased to say you have passed your lieutenants examination with flying colours. I hope your future is as interesting as your past."

"You are dismissed."

Marty saluted and turned to go when Cockburn said, "And please give my regards to Lady Caroline. She is my sister-in-law, you know."

Marty almost stumbled as he stopped and turned to see the captain grinning openly at him. Of the others, Pellew looked amused, Franklin and Lombard surprised, and Stonebridge just raised a single eyebrow.

After leaving the ship with his certificate amongst his papers, Marty collected his chest and Blaez from the inn he had left them at and caught the late post to London. He had a short argument with the driver about having a dog inside with him, but a crown ended that on a good note.

Once they arrived in London, he got a Hansom cab to Caroline's house. The greeting he received was, to say the least, demonstrative, passionate and extended. He forgot to ask about Cockburn and Blaez settled down in the kitchens, where he made himself very comfortable.

The next morning, he walked to the admiralty with Blaez on a lead, which he had made from some spare harness leather, and left the address where he could be contacted. Then he went to visit the de Marchets'.

After knocking on the door, he was shown into the drawing room by the butler, who told him the Count was with a visitor and would join him shortly. He stood in front of the fire, warming himself. After a few minutes, the door opened and the Count walked in, embraced him, and gave him a kiss on both cheeks.

"Mon cher, Martin," he said, "You look well. Admiral Hood told me you would be taking your lieutenants exams this week. How did they go?"

"I passed, thank you," Marty replied, "How is everybody? I was away for so long and the letters haven't caught up yet."

"Madam the Countess is well, she will be down soon so you can see her yourself. Evelyn is to marry her soldier boy, and young Antoine is growing fast and reading about all your adventures in your letters and the Gazette."

Marty felt a faint pang at the news that Evelyn would marry Arthur, but he had moved on and was in love with Caroline now. There, he had admitted it to himself.

There was the sound of running feet, the doors burst open, and Antoine rushed through yelling, "MARTY!"

Marty knelt down so that the ten-year-old boy could hug him then held him at arm's length. Blaez sniffed the boy then gave him a big wet lick, causing giggles.

"You have grown, Antoine," he said, "You will be big enough to go to sea soon." He looked up as the count coughed and saw the countess standing in the doorway looking horrified. He quickly stood and bowed, she embraced him.

"Please do not encourage him," she said, "he hero worships you, you know, and wants to go to sea as soon as he can."

"There are worse lives," Marty smiled.

"Marty has passed for lieutenant." Antoine crowed from where he was playing tug with the dog with one of the rope, curtain tiebacks.

"Congratulations, mon cher. When will you get a ship?" asked the countess deciding that the sacrifice of a curtain tie to distract her son was worth it.

"I will get the Lark as Armand has the Alouette," he replied, "and Tom and John Smith have been made warrant officers on her as well."

"Ha! And I wager that those Basque cut throats are on the crew as well," laughed the Count.

Marty just spread his hands and gave a "could I stop them?" look.

Marty changed the subject to Evelyn's wedding. It turned out that she would get married next summer at St. Martin-in-the-Fields. The bans were being read already.

"She is so excited," said the Countess, "you must come if you are home."

"Of course. I wouldn't miss it for the world if I am in port," he replied.

He stayed for lunch then making his excuses, walked back to Caroline's, which was less than a mile away.

He was in the library when she got home from a social visit with one of the many ladies' groups she attended.

"You didn't tell me Captain Cockburn was your brother-in-law." He mentioned over the top of the paper he was reading.

"He is married to my oldest sister, Julia. I didn't think to mention it."

"He was the chairman of the examination board. He sent his regards."

"Oh my! I hope it didn't disadvantage you!" she said in horror.

Marty laughed, "No. He is too smart to let that happen. He waited until the vote had been taken before he let it be known. All the same, I was surprised that it was public knowledge that we were seeing each other."

"Oh Marty," she smiled fondly, "you are so worldly but so innocent at the same time. After the duel, we were the main subject of gossip all over London and since then, we have been watched minutely. See here," she passed him a broadsheet.

He took a moment to find the item she was referring to and his eyebrows shot up in surprise and he said, "Oh my lord, I had no idea!"

What he read was a gossip column that purported to reveal the latest social news and scandal.

Lady Caroline Candor has most definitely broken all the hearts of the beaus that have been seeking her hand in marriage. She has been seen again with the dashing young Naval officer who fought a duel for her honour. The two lovebirds were arm in arm walking through Kensington, and a beautiful pair they make!

"Oh my God! I had no idea!" Marty cried, horrified at the exposure.

Caroline laughed and said,

"Don't worry, it's just noise to amuse the ladies who have nothing to do with their lives apart from gossip. It's not like being in the Gazette. That is really important."

When they went out to the Theatre the next evening, Marty couldn't help but feel as if everyone was watching him and he didn't like it, but Caroline's presence beside him more than made up for it.

Thursday morning, he was eating breakfast and feeding Blaez titbits of bacon and kidney when the butler brought an envelope on a silver tray and offered it to him. He immediately saw that the seal was the fouled anchor of the admiralty. In it were two large documents written in the traditional green ink and a note written in blue. The first document was his commission as a lieutenant and the second, his orders to take command of the Lark and to get her ready for sea by the end of the month. They were signed by the secretary to the First Naval Lord. The note was from Wickham asking him to attend him in Admiral Hood's office the next day at ten o'clock.

Caroline came in and asked what was in the letters. He told her, and she sat on his lap and kissed him soundly in congratulation.

"We must go shopping," she declared, "You need new uniforms and a dress sword," and then sat back and chewed her lip in thought.

Damn, she looks beautiful, Marty thought.

"We must also get furniture for your cabin, and you could do with a couple of new suits while we are at it. Shoes too and . . ." Marty shut her up with another kiss.

The rest of the day was spent at his tailor where he was measured for new uniforms and two suits styled in the latest fashion. Caroline insisted on buying him a dress sword, which was made by Wilkinson of Sheffield, and while they were in the shop, she also got him a set of seven shaving razors in a rosewood box, each marked with a day of the week. The shoes, she insisted, had to have silver buckles and he also had to have a new pair of hessian boots. She also got him a beautiful mahogany writing box fitted out with the latest pens. The furniture he chose was scaled to fit in the cabin of a Cutter and was plain, strongly built, and practical.

He asked for it all to be sent directly to the farm as he had a feeling he would be heading back to Kent fairly soon.

The next morning at ten minutes before ten, he was found in the waiting room of the admiralty, which had the usual selection of hopeful mids and lieutenants waiting for a berth on a ship. There were two, however, that caught his eye.

One was around five feet six or seven and stocky. He had broken his nose at some time, and it had a bit of a list to starboard. He had fair to mousy hair and blue eyes that had a direct look with an almost fierce intensity.

The other was tall with a shock of black hair, had broad shoulders, and exuded a physical presence. He noticed he had dark eyes that were verging on brooding and an almost Italian or Spanish cast to his features.

The clerk called out, "Lieutenant Stockley, Midshipman Campbell, and Midshipman Thompson."

Marty stepped forward and so did the two Mids. They looked at him in surprise as he was still wearing a midshipman's uniform.

They were led up the now familiar corridors to Admiral Hood's office and his secretary took them straight in. This time, there was a table set up with five chairs and Hood was sat at one end and Wickham at the other. Hood indicated that Marty should take the seat to his right as he greeted him.

"Congratulations, Mr. Stockley, on your promotion to lieutenant," Hood opened then looked him up and down.

"I trust you have ordered your new uniforms?" he added with an eye on Marty's attire.

"Thank you, my Lord, and yes, I visited my tailor yesterday," he replied.

"I'm sure Lady Caroline made sure you will go to sea well provisioned," smiled Wickham.

"Most probably, Sir," Marty grinned back at him.

"Now to business," interjected Hood, "Let me introduce you to Midshipmen Campbell and Thompson."

He pushed two dockets across to Marty. "Here are summaries of their careers to date. You can read them later."

Wickham looked up and said, "Suffice for now is that they have both shown they are proficient in their duties as midshipmen and have shown particular talents for the kind of tasks that we undertake. Mr. Campbell," he nodded to the shorter of the two, "speaks French, thanks to a French mother, and has shown an adventurous spirit having been kicked off his last ship for being involved in a professional bare-knuckle fight in the Haymarket."

Marty looked at him closely and could see the signs of scarring around the eyebrows that a fist fighter would get.

"Mr. Thompson," Wickham continued, "has had to leave his ship after being caught with the captain's daughter in the cockpit." Marty could see Wickham was suppressing a smile.

"Captain Lombard has agreed to leave it to me to see that Mr. Thompson is sufficiently punished," added Hood, "and I thought a couple of years with you and Armand would be sufficient."

"Mr. Thompson also speaks fluent Italian," continued Wickham, looking slightly annoyed at the interruption, "and has a working knowledge of Spanish."

"We can probably teach them everything else they will need to know," Marty concluded. "Have they been sworn to secrecy?"

"Yes, they have," Wickham said.

"Do we have any special operations to perform in the near future?" Marty asked and both mids looked surprised at him speaking so.

"We have one that we are considering for the new year, but it will depend on what Napoleon does once he gets back from Egypt," Wickham said.

"In the meantime, you have time to get your new crews into order and disrupt the flow of goods from the Americas to the French," Hood concluded.

"Keep those pirates of yours under control, especially the Deal fellows. They have been flooding the market with quality brandy and wine and the excise are up in arms over their protection."

Marty frowned in thought and then said, "what if we were to pay an 'import tax' would that make them happier?"

"Might ease the situation a bit but it's the basic principle of allowing the smuggling to go on in the first place that has their noses out of joint," Wickham said.

The meeting broke up at that point, and Marty walked out of the Admiralty with the two mids in tow. He ordered them to meet him outside of Caroline's house at 06:00 the next morning with their sea chests as they would journey with him to the farm.

When he told Caroline he would be leaving in the morning, she wasn't surprised and told him he could use one of her coaches. She said that she would visit him as soon as she could get away, but as Christmas was looming, there was a lot she needed to organize both in London and at her estate. That night, neither got a lot of sleep.

The next morning at six o'clock saw him and Blaez in the hallway watching as his sea chest was taken by a pair of servants out the front door. Caroline was in a silk dressing gown, and he knew not a lot else, looking sleepy but determined to see him off. She held him close, kissed him thoroughly, and made him promise to be careful. Blaez pushed his nose between them and whined, getting all jealous. She stood back and let him jump up for a cuddle and a scratch around his neck and told him sternly, "You look after Marty now; he is your responsibility," Blaez rolled his eyes then licked her from the base of her throat to her chin. "I'll take that as a yes," she giggled.

"I have to go," Marty said. Caroline took his arm, led him to the door, and opened it. The morning air was freezing, and she hugged him one more time and kissed him before saying "I'm going back to bed." She looked towards the coach and saw the two mids standing there with their mouths open. She gave them a wicked grin then kissed Marty on the nose and ducked inside. It was as she was retreating that Marty noticed the dressing gown did nothing to hide her figure. Damn, he was a lucky man.

"What you two gawping at," he snarled "Get yerselves loaded and be quick about it."

He got in last and Blaez curled up on the seat next to him, giving the mids an 'I dare you to say anything' look. He looked up to the window of Caroline's bedroom and saw her looking down at him. He smiled and touched his hat to her. "Move out coachman!" he called, and they were on their way.

Epilogue

After Marty and the two mids left the office, Hood and Wickham each took a comfortable chair beside the large fire.

"The boy is coming on well," Wickham commented, sipping a cup of coffee.

"Yes, flew through his exam and was the best of the bunch," replied Hood.

"Did you plant Cockburn on the board?" asked Wickham.

"No. Lucky coincidence. I planted Pellew," Hood laughed.

Wickham chuckled at that.

"Mind you, starting out with a merchantman and coming home with a corvette didn't hurt his prospects," Hood stated.

They sat drinking their coffee for a few minutes in silence.

"Do you think he will be ready for a tougher mission in the new year?" he asked.

"Linette says he is the best she has worked with. Creative, ruthless, and deadly. He killed a secret policeman, and the poor fellow didn't even realise he had been stabbed until he died. Yes, I think he can handle one, even Paris," Wickham answered. "What about the two new boys?"

"Armand and Martin will make them or break them. They have the potential, but we will have to see if they shape up to what we want," Hood answered.

"If they fail, they will have to 'disappear'," Wickham said.

"If they fail, they will be dead anyway," Hood responded.

"Fancy a Brandy in that?"

THANK YOU FOR READING!

I hope you enjoyed reading this book as much as I enjoyed writing it. Reviews are so helpful to authors. I really appreciate all reviews, both positive and negative. If you want to leave one, you can do so on Amazon or through the website or Twitter.

About the Author

Christopher C Tubbs is a descendent of a long line of Dorset clay miners and has chased his family tree back to the 16th century in the Isle of Purbeck. He has been a public speaker at conferences for most of his career in the Aerospace and Automotive industries and was one of the founders of a successful games company back in the 1990's. Now, just turned sixty, he finally got around to writing the story he had been dreaming about for years. Thanks to Inspiration from the great sea authors like Alexander Kent, Dewey Lambdin, Patrick O'Brian and Dudley Pope he was finally able to put digit to keyboard. He lives in the Netherlands with his wife, two Dutch Shepherds and a Norwegian Forest cat.

You can visit him on his website

www.thedorsetboy.com

Or tweet him @ChristopherCTu3

And Now!

Preview of Book 3, Agent Provocateur.

Chapter 1 - Reading In

Newly commissioned Lieutenant Martin Stockley stood in front of a long mirror in his room at the headquarters of the Special Operations Flotilla, or The Farm as they called it, and admired the fit of the new Uniform that had just arrived from his tailor in London. He was trying to decide whether to wear his silver buckled shoes or hessian boots when there was a knock on the door.

"Come in." he called

Will Barbour their steward entered and said,

"Oh Sir, you do look proper good. Suits you to a tee. Mr Armand said if you could hurry up as they is all waiting on yer."

Shoes it is then Marty concluded and pulled on one of his three new pairs. The men had asked if they could celebrate his promotion with a dinner and 'a few wets', which meant they were in for a wild time this evening. Sailors seldom did just 'a few wets' and had a prodigious capacity for alcohol.

The Deal smugglers were ready to supply the best brandy and wines to them for free as the S.O.F. were their protection and the source of most of their wealth. Bill their leader and his lieutenants had been invited as well. This evening would be long, merry and test the stamina of the strongest.

Marty entered the large dining room to a roar of congratulation. He made a show of acknowledging the cheers and then struck a pose. He waited until they quieted.

"Thank you, thank you, thank you." He said to the left centre and right in turn as he looked around the room registering the faces. "I understand that Monsieur du Demaine has taken over the kitchens for this celebration so I am sure we will all eat well!"

Another cheer!

This would not go down well at the Admiralty! He thought and he was right the Admiralty would have a very dim view of the familiarity between the men and officers. But this was the S.O.F. and things worked differently here.

Let them enjoy themselves he thought I will break the bad news about the next mission later.

The next morning, despite hangovers, they ordered the Lark and Alouette to be prepared for a six-week voyage. They would go hunting neutral ships supplying goods to the French in opposition to any agreements their governments may have with the British.

Marty left for the dock to check on progress and to read himself in as the Lark's official commander. He was dressed in his best uniform and hat and wore the dress sword that the love of his life, Lady Caroline Candor, had given him. As he walked up to the dock he thought it ironic that his cutter and the sloop moored next to her shared the same name in two languages at times. But this morning the Alouette was called the Swan as she was in English waters.

It was a fine morning, although very cold, and he enjoyed the short walk from The Farm to the dock on the river Stour where their three craft were moored. He soon warmed up and his breath steamed. Blaez, his young Dutch Shepherd dog, trotted along with him checking out the verges for any trace of either intruding dogs or receptive bitches and marking his territory at regular intervals.

He arrived at the dock to find it a hive of activity. Wagons were lined up ready to unload food and other dry stores into nets which were hoisted aboard and down into the hold. This was faster and needed less men than forming chain gangs. Water barrels were being loaded into empty wagons to be filled from a spring a short ride away as the river water was brackish this close to the sea.

He didn't notice the elegant coach tucked away behind one of the storage sheds as he only had eyes for his ship.

He walked up the gang plank on to the deck of the Cutter that was his first command as a Lieutenant. She was a little beauty with her long, elegant bowsprit, which was almost half as long as her hull, and single mast. She was normally gaff rigged with multiple fore sails that gave her fantastic manoeuvrability but could carry a couple of square sails if she needed to swim downwind as well.

She was armed with ten, twenty-four-pound carronades which gave her a close in punch that was far heavier than anyone would expect and when she was fought in consort with the Alouette they could give a nasty surprise to anyone who took them on. The advantage of the carronades was that they only needed four men each to man them or three in a pinch. But their short range could put you in trouble if up against guns with longer range.

The men smiled at him as he made his way aft to the wheel and Blaez greeted many of them with a headbutt and a lick. When he got to Tom he reared up on his hind legs and planted them on his chest, looked him straight in the eye and licked him from the base of his neck to the tip of his chin. Marty laughed at that and from the soppy look on Tom's face.

He beckoned Midshipman Campbell over and asked him to assemble the men on the main deck and when they had settled, he took out his commission and started to read.

"By the Commissioners for executing the Office of the Lord High Admiral of Great Britain &c and of all His Majesty's Plantations &c.

To Lieut. Martin Alfred Stockley hereby appointed Master and Commander of His Majesty's Ship Snipe.

By virtue of the Power and Authority to us given We do hereby constitute and appoint you Master and Commander of His Majesties Ship Snipe willing and requiring you forthwith to go on board and take upon you the Charge and Command of Master and Commander in her accordingly. Strictly Charging and Commanding all the Officers and Company belonging to the said ship subordinate to you to behave themselves jointly and severally in their respective Employments with all the Respect and Obedience unto you their said Master and Commander; And you likewise to observe and execute as well the General printed Instructions as what Orders and Directions you shall from time to time receive from your superior Officers for His Majesty's service. Hereof nor you nor any of you may fail as you will answer the contrary at your peril. And for so doing this shall be your Warrant. Given under our hands and the Seal of the Office Admiralty this 20th day of September in the one thousandth seven hundredth and ninety eighth Year of His Majesty's Reign.

By Command of their Lordships"

He reached the end and looked up. He was faced with a sea of smiling, but expectant, faces. *Oh shit, they want me to make a speech!* He thought in panic. His brain went into fast mode like he was in combat.

"Looking around all your faces," he swept his gaze over the men and stopped in astonishment. There dressed as a common sailor was Caroline?

He coughed to cover the gap.

"I see many who have sailed and fought with me in the past and some new ones."

He pointedly didn't look at Caroline.

"Well, you old hands can tell the new hands what to expect. But one thing I will tell all of you is that you can all expect to continue doing the jobs that no one else wants, in ways no one else will. We are the S.O.F. We will bring pain and confusion to the French and anyone who sides with them." He paused to look around again

"And if we are lucky make a few bob for ourselves." He concluded causing a chuckle.

He raised his hat to the men and stepped back signifying he had finished.

The deck erupted in cheers when someone who sounded very much like John Smith called "Three Cheers and a Tiger for the skipper!"

Marty waited until the cheers died down and then said "Right, now get back to work you idle lubbers. There is no excuse to be shirking!"

To Tom he said.

"And I want to see the sailor with the auburn hair and green eyes in my cabin as soon as you can find her"

Books by Christopher C Tubbs

The Dorset Boy Series.

A Talent for Trouble

The Special Operations Flotilla

Agent Provocateur

In Dangerous Company

The Tempest

Vendetta

The Trojan Horse

La Licorne

Raider

Silverthorn

Exile

The Scarlet Fox Series

Scarlett

A Kind of Freedom

Legacy

See them all at:

Website: www.thedorsetboy.com

Twitter: @ChristoherCTu3

Facebook: https://www.facebook.com/thedorsetboy/

YouTube: https://youtu.be/KCBR4ITqDi4

Published in E-Book, Paperback and Audio formats on Amazon, Audible and iTunes

Printed in Great Britain
by Amazon

54291553R00148